SAFE & SOUND

LINDY ZART

Safe and Sound
Lindy Zart
Published by Lindy Zart
Copyright 2012 Lindy Zart
Cover design 2014 by Sprinkles On Top
Studios Formatted by Inkstain Interior Book
Author Photography by Kelley C. Hanson
Designing All rights reserved.
This book is a work of fiction. Names, characters, places, and incidents either are products of the author's imagination or are used fictitiously. Any resemblance to actual events or locales or persons, living or dead, is entirely coincidental.

—Special thanks to Jessie Schwarz and Wendi Stitzer,
for helping me out with a few questions I had.
Any mistakes are mine.

—For Jamie and Joshua

SAFE & SOUND

CHAPTER 1

ONLY IN THE SOLITUDE OF her mind did she truly find peace.

Lola had realized something lately—she was better off when she didn't have to worry about what anyone else thought about her or how she should think about them. Not that anyone really wanted to know about her problems anyway. Sure, they acted concerned, but as soon as she began to talk, they changed the subject, their eyes glazed over. They turned away. Lately whenever anyone asked how she was doing, Lola smiled and said everything was okay. Even if it wasn't.

And it never was.

She blinked her burning eyes and slammed the locker door shut. Kids hurried up and down the hall, eager to get out of the stuffy brick building. Voices overlapped until it was one loud buzzing noise in her ears. Cologne and perfume and body odor polluted the air. She hunched her shoulders and lowered her head, trying not to draw attention to herself as she walked down the corridor.

It was a small school, as Morgan Creek, Wisconsin was a microscopic town with a population under two thousand. There were less than one hundred kids in each grade, and yet still enough to make the hallway crowded as she maneuvered her way outside. Life was so much different now than it used to be. Last year she would have been in that crowd of kids, laughing and talking. This year she tried to avoid them.

The thought of going home made her stomach queasy. She sucked in a ragged breath of the cool spring air and squinted against the bright day her pale blue eyes were forever sensitive to. She should have learned by now to carry sunglasses with her. One more thing she couldn't seem to do right.

She was jostled from behind and tightened her grip on the backpack strap as she kept walking. The nudge could have been purposeful or it could have been an accident. It could have been from someone she knew or someone she didn't. Either way, she pretended not to notice.

Tree limbs swayed in the breeze, showing off their new green leaves. She turned down the sidewalk toward home, footsteps echoing her own. She glanced behind her, her pace unconsciously slowing. Sebastian averted his eyes and rushed past when she paused. He didn't say anything, didn't acknowledge her in any way.

Lola stared after his tall, lanky frame, wondering why it still hurt so much. They hadn't spoken in close to a year, not since before her seventeenth birthday. One year was enough time to move on, to forget the pain, to get over a lost friendship. Why did her chest and throat still tighten every time he brushed by her? Every time their eyes met and his slid away?

She swallowed. The house before her blurred and she blinked until it came into focus. It was a tan ranch-style with brown trim. The grass was overgrown and ready for its first cut of the year. A fold-up chair lay on its side near a towering pine tree. The lawn used to be well-kept with cute outdoor décor to brighten the place up. That was all in the past.

She slowly made her way to the door, her racing pulse at odds with her movements. Lola went through a mental list in her head, trying to think of what she may or may not have done to cause his anger. With her hand on the cool door handle, she looked over her shoulder to the house across the street. Sebastian stood there, hands in his jeans pockets. He watched her, his expression blank. The wind ran invisible fingers through his light brown hair, tousling it. When their gazes locked he turned away and went inside.

Lola had no choice but to do so as well.

She took a deep breath and quietly opened the door, wrinkling her nose upon entering. It smelled like unwashed bodies and fried food. The living room was dark, but the television was on with the volume turned low. She found the remote under an old newspaper and turned the TV off.

The house had once been spotless and smelled of whatever cake or cookies her mother was baking when she got home from school. Now it was dirty except for when Lola cleaned, and there was no baking. Other than glimpses of and shortly held conversations, there was no mother either. She inhaled sharply against the pain in her chest.

She righted a pillow, straightened magazines on the coffee table. Lola folded a blanket and put it on the arm of the tan recliner, moving on to open the windows to allow fresh air in. She sprayed fabric freshener on the furniture and started to vacuum.

"What the hell are you doing?" a low voice growled in her ear.

She jumped and fumbled with the off switch on the vacuum cleaner, backpedaling away from Bob until her back hit the wall. "Nothing," she was quick to answer.

Bob was over six feet tall and burly. He had a gut that hung over his pants from all the beer he drank. His black hair was thinning and there was a perpetual sheen of oil to his skin that showed how much he thought about personal hygiene. His features were plain, but the ever-present sneer on his lips and unkind gleam in his small brown eyes boasted his sinister nature. He had on a stained white tee shirt and his pale, hairy legs could be seen below his red boxers.

He punched the vacuum cleaner to the floor with a beefy fist. "It doesn't look like *nothing*." He advanced on her, the smell of unwashed skin amplifying. "Are you lying to me, girl?"

She shook her head, strands of auburn hair sticking to her flushed cheeks. "No! I was just...just cleaning." She pressed her back flat to the wall, wanting to sink into it and away from him.

Bob put his face close to hers, his breath hot and putrid. She turned her head to the side and squeezed her eyes shut. "So you *were* lying. You said you were doing nothing and you were doing something."

Her stomach turned as his breath hit her. "Please," she whispered.

He shoved away from the wall. "Your mother is trying to sleep. In case you forgot, she works third shift. Keep it down." He shook a finger at her. "No vacuuming."

"No vacuuming. Sorry. I should have known that."

His lips twisted and he ambled from the room, kicking over a soda can as he went. Fizzy brown liquid soaked through the carpet in an uneven circle.

She went to her knees, anger and fear and relief warring inside her. She hated Bob—she was also terribly scared of him. Her body trembled and tears seeped from the corners of her eyes, dropping to her lap. At times like this, she almost hated her mother as much as him. How could she allow this to happen?

A sob escaped her and she put a hand to her mouth to keep it in, slowly getting to her feet. She took a deep, calming breath. And another. This time wasn't so bad. It could have been worse. With that thought in her mind, Lola cleaned up the spilled soda.

SAFE & SOUND

HER BEDROOM WAS HER SAFE haven, the one place in the whole house where she wasn't afraid. The room she spent as much time in as she could when she had to be at 310 Sycamore Drive. She sat on her bed with the pink and white polka dot bedspread she and her mother picked out together. Before. She ran a hand across the soft material, sadness washing over her. That's how she defined her life now—with before. And after. Then. And now.

The bedroom was big enough for the daybed, dresser, and computer desk, but not much more. A full-length mirror hung on the back of the door. She and her mother painted the walls lavender. The lone window in the room had iridescent curtains that shimmered in rainbow colors when the sun shone. Everything in the room had been done pre Bob Holden. It had been so long ago some days all those happy memories seemed like they had all been nothing but a dream—or like they were someone else's and she'd merely caught glimpses of them through a window. All the laughter and smiles shared with her mom; maybe none of it had ever happened. Maybe it was all in her head and now was the reality and always had been.

Her mother met Bob when he started working third shift at Ray-O-Vac, the factory outside of town that made batteries. At first he hadn't seemed so bad. At first Lola had thought everything might be okay. As soon as he'd moved in, he'd gotten mean. And once he and her mother married, he'd gotten even meaner. It started out with a teasing comment that wasn't exactly teasing, ridicule, a criticism, and escalated into physical and mental abuse. A pinch here, a shove there, a slap across the face, name calling. And what had her mother done about it? *Nothing*. She had done nothing and she continued to do nothing. She acted like she didn't know it was going on, but how could she *not*?

A knock sounded at the door and she scrambled to her feet, her pulse immediately racing. *Please don't be him.*

"Lola?"

The door opened and there stood a washed-out version of Lana Murphy; now Lana Holden. She wore a red shirt that went to her knees and black pajama pants. Her auburn hair was dull and showed gray. Her pale blue eyes were tired and shadows had found a home beneath them. Her stooped shoulders made her seem shorter than her five feet six inches and her body was thin to the point of being unhealthy. This wasn't supposed to be her mother and Lola stared at her, having trouble putting the person she remembered with the person that stood before her. It physically hurt Lola to look at her. It was her mom, but it wasn't. The changes had been so gradual that she hadn't noticed them until one day she'd looked at her sad, worn-out mother and hadn't recognized her. It was still a shock to her eyes each time they rested on her.

She stayed by her bed, keeping her distance. "Hi, Mom."

Lana's lips turned up in a fleeting smile. "Hi, honey. Did you start supper?"

Her skin flushed and she looked at the glowing red numbers of the alarm clock on the stand beside her bed. "Of course I did. I do every night, don't I?"

Her mother's face fell and Lola's chest constricted. She didn't want to hurt her, not really, but she was hurting too. She looked down so she didn't have to see the pain in her mother's eyes.

"Thank you for that. I'm just so tired all the time." She lifted a hand to her limp hair and let it fall to her side. "I don't know what's wrong with me," she mumbled, turning away.

Lola wanted to scream at her, to shake her. She wanted to throw something, to hit the wall with all the helpless rage pulling her under. Anything to get her attention, to force her to wake up. *You know what's wrong and you do nothing about it!*

Her hands fisted as she clenched her teeth. The words she so desperately wanted to shout would have no effect on her mother except to make her sad. And then Bob would get involved. Lola knew from experience. So she bit her tongue, like she always did, and said nothing.

LOLA WORKED MOST NIGHTS AT Granger's, the local grocery store in Morgan Creek. Three to four hours at the cash register on weeknights and usually six hours either Saturday or Sunday, but sometimes both days. It was how she paid for her clothes and whatever else she wanted that Bob didn't consider a necessity. She had been saving up for a car and had close to one thousand dollars in her savings account. Another thousand and she would have enough to get a somewhat decent car.

The temperature in the store was kept cool and by the registers it smelled of cleaning solution. Low music played from speakers in the ceiling, adding a touch of livelihood to the otherwise lifeless atmosphere. Everyone sort of walked around like a zombie, even on busy days. Lola never understood that—the faster you moved, the quicker you got stuff done. The wall near the registers was made up of windows. It was odd to look out at the black night from the brightly lit interior; it was like a different world out there full of darkness and the unknown—or just the quiet streets of Morgan Creek.

It was nine-thirty and she had half an hour left to go before the store closed. It was slow and she and the other two cashiers passed the time by talking to one another. Well, they talked, and she listened.

"Lola, you're quiet tonight. What's the matter?" Dorothy asked in her loud voice.

Her face burned. She wasn't being any quieter than any other night, but as Dorothy needed constant chatter, she could see how she would come to such a conclusion. She turned her head and looked up from the uneven fingernail she'd been staring at, finding two pairs of eyes set on her.

Dorothy Dean was in her fifties, plump, and had a laugh that made others around her want to laugh as well. She was retired and said she worked part-time at the store so she didn't go completely nuts from boredom at home. Her green top and black slacks clung to her body, her gray hair was short and spiky. The green eyes presently locked on her always seemed to dance and Lola found herself smiling more than usual in her company.

But not tonight.

"Nothing. Everything's fine." She even managed a brief smile, though it felt forced. It *was* forced.

She narrowed her eyes and pursed her lips. "I'm a mother. I know when something's not right with a child. What is it?"

She bit her lip and looked away. It wasn't any new thing that was wrong, just an accumulation of it all. Dorothy's kindness cut through her like a blade of empathy. What she wouldn't give for her mother to acknowledge something wasn't right. Lana was in denial. Lola knew that. It was Bob's word against hers and Lola's didn't matter.

She felt like nothing; like she was nothing and meant nothing to her mother.

"I'm fine," she said in a shaky voice.

"She's always like that, Dot, you know that," Roxanne said. "Might as well save your breath and not bother talking to her."

She bristled, but kept her back to them.

"Roxanne. You hush," Dorothy admonished.

Roxanne Zanders was a year ahead of Lola in school. She was also most recently Sebastian Jones' girlfriend. Lola didn't like her, but that wasn't why. She didn't like her because she was manipulative, sneaky, and mean. To her, anyway. She didn't know what she was like to other people and she didn't care. She just knew that every chance she got, she made sure Lola felt inferior in some way.

Sebastian's girlfriend was tall, slender, had flaming red hair, and just as red lips. Freckles spattered her pale skin, somehow adding to her cold beauty. Her eyes were an unusual shade of green—close to lime—and flashed with dislike whenever they encountered her. She had a perfect body and liked to show it off in tight, short clothing. Even her work outfit molded to her lithe frame in a positive way.

Lola may have had a good body at one point, but it was too thin now. She didn't eat much because her stomach was upset all of the time. She carried a roll of Tums around in her purse, but they didn't do much. It was an emotional problem, not clinical. She knew most girls her age would love to be in such a predicament that it was hard to overindulge in food, but she would trade with them without hesitation to be able to eat a large burger and fries without worrying about throwing it back up.

"I'm just stating a fact," Roxanne said.

"Facts aren't always nice, nor do they always need to be stated," Dorothy retorted.

Lola's lips curved up and a small, but significant weight lifted. She looked at her and mouthed, "Thank you."

A few customers straggled through her checkout lane and the store closed for the night. She went about her closing duties with the register, pulled on her white hooded sweatshirt, and grabbed her purse. She shivered in the chilly night air, wishing it would warm up so she didn't have to freeze walking home at night. Street lamps offered a little light in the parking lot, but not much. Two cars were in the parking lot; one a blue Nissan and the other a silver Pontiac.

Dorothy squeezed her shoulder as she passed. "You have a good night, sweetheart. Don't let Roxanne get to you."

She knew it was stupid and weak of her, but her eyes pricked at the thoughtful gesture. She watched as Dorothy contorted her large frame into her little blue car and drove off.

The door opened to the other car and Sebastian got out. For one brief, dizzying moment, she thought he was there for her. Then reality set in. Roxanne brushed past, bumping her shoulder, and skipped over to him. She flung her arms around him and kissed him long and hard, most likely for her benefit. Lola felt sick and turned away.

She began to walk toward home. Her mother didn't have to be to work until eleven, but she never offered to pick her up. And the one time she asked, Bob ridiculed her so badly she never asked again. She kicked at a rock with her tennis shoe. Lola walked to and from work in the winter, in the spring, in the summer, and in the fall. No matter the weather—no matter how cold or hot it was. She was like a United States postal worker.

Sebastian's car slowed beside her, but she refused to acknowledge its presence. The window rolled down and warm air taunted her cold body. "Need a ride?" Roxanne asked, not sounding the least bit happy about it.

"No," she bit out, teeth chattering.

Only six blocks to go. If you get too cold, you can run them. She didn't want a ride from them, especially if Sebastian was so chicken he made his girlfriend ask; his girlfriend that *loathed* her. *One more reason for her to hate me. Great.*

"She said no. Let's go. Come *on*, Sebastian."

She kept her eyes trained ahead, wishing they would leave. She hunched her shoulders against the cold. What she wouldn't give for a scarf or gloves. Winter was supposedly over, but maybe someone should have told April that. She didn't realize the car had stopped until a door slammed.

Lola halted only when Sebastian placed himself directly in her path. His hair was windswept and he wore dark jeans, a black leather bomber jacket, and black boots. His jaw was clenched in that stubborn way of his, his brows lowered over stormy gray eyes.

Her breath caught. She'd forgotten how stunning he was up close, especially when he turned his intense gaze on her.

"Get in the car, Lola," he said in a low voice.

She lifted her chin, though her body quaked. "No."

It had been so long since he'd talked to her, so long since he'd spoken her name. A tidal wave of conflicting emotions crashed over her; the most prominent one resentment. Lola didn't know what she'd done to make him stop speaking to her. She didn't know why he'd decided not to be her friend anymore. She'd *needed* him. She'd needed him to be her friend; he'd been her closest friend, and he'd just...*left her.* He'd abandoned her. When she'd needed him the most, he wasn't there. Sebastian never even had the decency to explain *why*.

It hurt.

"Sebastian, really? She said *no*. I'm cold and I'm tired and I don't have *time* for this."

They stared at each other, not speaking. She put everything she was feeling into her eyes and she hoped he choked on what he saw.

He finally looked away, but it didn't last long. When he turned back, there was renewed determination etched into his features. "It's thirty degrees out. You can't walk home. Get in the car."

"You have no manners. And you're bossy. I never realized that before. Better now than never, right?"

His jaw clenched and he took a quick step toward her. She took one back. He stopped and narrowed his eyes at her.

"Sebastian!" A car door slammed and Roxanne stormed over, putting herself between them. She gave Lola a look that blazed with animosity. *I will get you for this*, those eyes promised. She crossed her arms. "She doesn't want a ride. She said so herself." She turned to Lola. "*Right*, Lola? You don't want a ride." *Agree, or I will make your life hell*, she said without uttering a single word.

She looked Sebastian in the eye, something he hadn't allowed for close to a year. She wondered what had changed. Lola decided it didn't matter. "Right."

Roxanne grabbed his arm and tugged. "Come on. My parents are going to be pissed if I'm not home in about two minutes."

He didn't budge, his eyes like laser beams of heat on her skin. He pressed his lips together and finally turned away. Relief and sorrow simultaneously hit Lola.

With a satisfied look on her face, Roxanne skipped back to the car.

Lola watched him go, surprised when Sebastian turned back around and stopped beside her, his face forward. She stiffened, heart racing.

"How long have you been walking home at night?"

She looked straight ahead as well, focusing on a dark building across the street. "As long as I've worked here, Sebastian," she answered tiredly.

"How long have you worked here?"

"Eight months."

"That's..." He broke off. "That's not safe."

Her skin heated up. Why did he suddenly care? "Don't worry about it. It's none of your concern. Besides, nothing bad ever happens in a small town like Morgan Creek, right?" she said bitterly. *Nothing anyone wants to know about anyway.*

"Se-*bast*-ian!"

He let out a sigh. "She is driving me *crazy*," he muttered.

She fought an impulse to smile. "You better go." Out of the corner of her eye she caught his nod.

She tried to squash the empty feeling that reared up as soon as the Pontiac's taillights disappeared around the corner of the building. He'd acted like he actually cared about her, about what happened to her. Lola shook her head. He didn't. A year of silence had proven that. Actions always spoke louder than words. She'd learned that the hard way. Many times.

It was hard to believe they were the way they were now; barely speaking and uncomfortable in each other's company. They used to be so close. Lola was at his house all the time; his mother and father had been like her surrogate parents and she like a daughter to them. A lot had been better just a short time ago. All of it before Bob had entered her life and snuffed out all the joy like a dark cloud of doom.

When she reached her house, cold and beyond tired, she unconsciously turned to the buttercup yellow two-story house across the street. She always did that, no matter how many times she told herself not to. Expecting to find the yard empty, she stumbled when her eyes made out the tall figure of a man standing in the grass. Her heart squeezed.

She quickly turned away and hurried to the door. She looked back one last time as she reached it. Sebastian's hand lifted and dropped as he walked toward his house. Lola leaned her hot forehead against the cold door. A spark of hope fought to bloom within her and she wouldn't allow it to. One second of being polite to her did not make up for the thick wedge of months spent ignoring her.

BREAKFAST DISHES WASHED AND PUT away, Lola went about sweeping the kitchen floor. She'd made pancakes she and her mother both picked at and Bob complained were too chewy, though he'd eaten six of them. She'd gotten the wrong kind of orange juice too; the kind she *always* got, but *today* it had been the wrong kind.

The kitchen was painted a cheery yellow and accented in red checkered curtains and apples galore. It used to be her favorite place to be. She and her mother would bake cookies together and talk about silly things, giggling and happy. She and Sebastian would do their homework at the table. Rachel, another friend she'd lost touch with, used to gossip with her about boys and girls over PB and J's and milk. Things had been pretty wonderful just a year ago. Such a short amount of time, really, and yet it seemed the year since Bob showed up had been never-ending.

Now there was a gash in the cherry wood table from Bob's steak knife from the time Lola had overcooked his steak and burned the potatoes. It had been a small rebellion on her part that had led to food being splattered across the wall, the gash in the table, a broken plate, and her mother's tears.

"What are you doing?" Bob demanded from the doorway. He wore a blue flannel shirt with holes in it, only partially buttoned, and gray sweat pants. He had never been a handsome man, but for a time he'd been groomed and clean; now he was just disgusting in smell and looks. Her skin crawled. How could her mother stand his touch?

Lola jumped, dropping the broom. She quickly picked it up and faced him. "Sweeping."

He moved into the room and grabbed the broom from her. "You can't even sweep right. *This* is how you sweep."

She watched him push the broom back and forth across the floor. How could there be a wrong way to sweep?

"See?"

She nodded, though his way of sweeping and her way of sweeping looked quite similar. And she'd swept that floor a million times since he'd been married to her mother and he'd never once complained about the way she swept before. But of course she couldn't say any of that. Lola used to. She used to say things.

He shoved the broom at her and she fumbled to grasp it. "I'm taking your mother grocery shopping. Did you make a list like I told you? With the right kind of orange juice written down?"

She nodded again, wanting so badly for him to just go away.

Bob put a hand to his ear and cocked his head. "I can't hear you."

"Yes."

"Where is it?"

"On the counter."

His eyes drilled into hers and Lola shifted, wanting to run from the room. "Get. It." She didn't move fast enough and he pinched her arm. "*Now.*"

She darted to the counter and plucked the small sheet of paper from it, outstretching her hand with her head down. He snatched it from her fingers and she quickly pulled her hand away.

Bob feinted toward her with his fist raised and she jerked back, her face heating as he laughed. "Not so tough, are ya?"

Lola stared at the back of his head as he walked from the room, anger and hate burning through her. She could see herself grab a large pot and bash him over the head with it. She could hear the satisfying thud as metal met flesh. She could see him fall to the floor, unconscious and maybe dead. And she was *happy*. She shook the upsetting thought away and swept the floor with renewed vigor.

CHAPTER 2

LOLA ZIPPED HER JACKET AND quietly left the house, clutching a purple folder to her chest. A cool breeze blew her hair over her eyes and she pushed it away. The sun was bright, warming her where it touched her. The air was cleansing and she inhaled deeply. Her eyes strayed to the house across the street, not surprised to find it silent and still. It was early Saturday morning, not even eight yet. Lola had to work at noon and wanted to take advantage of the hours before then.

She turned in the direction of the park. It was a short walk, taking her less than five minutes to get there. The park had full green grass, lots of shady trees, and play equipment she and Sebastian used to play on as kids. It seemed almost every memory she had of her childhood involved Sebastian. There was a shelter mainly used for family get-togethers and a basketball court high school boys liked to monopolize.

Lola found a bench and sat down. Inside the folder she opened were pages and pages of words, some flowing, others erratic, some that didn't even make sense to her once she went back and read them. The one constant with all of them, though, was the despair—

that didn't change from poem to poem. She found one she'd written over six months ago. Her hand paused, and then pulled it from the folder. Her eyes blurred as she read:

The Truth
Try to convince yourself you're sane, try to overcome the pain.
You may feel like dying, but you can't stop trying.
If you look hard enough, you'll find a friend.
If you pray long enough, you'll learn to trust again.
True, you have been hurt. Yes, you are confused.
But you have to face the fact:
you didn't deserve to be abused.

A sob escaped her and Lola put a hand over her mouth, eyes searching for possible witnesses. She didn't want anyone to see her weep. It was bad enough she had a tendency to do so on a whim these days; it would be worse if someone saw it.

Don't cry. Stop crying. Don't cry.

Her eyes burned with the need to release her pain. Reading those words was like reliving the fear and sense of helplessness of every cruel action or word Bob had ever inflicted on her. She took a deep breath and shoved the paper back into the folder. Blank sheet of paper before her, pen in hand, Lola chewed her lower lip as she tried to put her current emotions into words.

Acceptance
She's dead, I thought. How can she be dead?
Then I remembered all the pain she'd endured throughout her life and I understood. Physically she was not dead, but her soul was. She just sat there with a lifeless look in her eyes and lived in her own world. In her safe haven, there was no emotion, only acceptance.
She glanced up in sorrow and...

I gazed at myself through a dusty window.

Lola stared at the words. It was funny how almost every poem she wrote started out about her or her mother and somewhere during the process turned out being about the opposite one. Or maybe they all were about them both. Their life hadn't been perfect. There had been clashes of will and temper tantrums and whatever else was normal between a parent and their child. But there hadn't been abuse. Her mother hadn't locked herself in her room all the time and slept.

Or had she?

She tried to think back. Maybe occasionally her mother had had days like that, but not *every* day. There had forever been a sadness to her mother's eyes because of the husband she'd lost, but she'd still managed to *function*, to be a mother to Lola. Now she wasn't anything.

Sneakers thudded against the pavement and Lola jerked her head toward the basketball court, dismayed to see Sebastian. He had on black athletic shorts and a matching jacket, his hair a darker shade of brown with wetness. His eyes were on her, studying and searching, his hand dribbling a basketball with the ease of a natural athlete.

"Hey."

Lola turned her head away and slammed the folder full of her writing shut, getting to her feet.

"Lola, wait."

She spun around and glared at him. "Are we suddenly on speaking terms again? I guess I didn't get the memo."

He was close, too close, and she took a step back. Even with the added distance between them, she could smell him. He smelled like toothpaste and deodorant and soap. He smelled familiar, good. Her chest ached and she fought the urge to cry. She missed her friend, she missed him so much.

He looked down at the ball in his large hands. When had his hands gotten so big? And his shoulders bulked out? His cheekbones were more hollowed out, his chin squarer than she remembered. He was a young man now, no longer a boy. Sebastian would be eighteen in less than a month. How had a year physically changed him so much? Lola thought of how much she had visually metamorphosed in the last year and knew it wasn't so unimaginable, not really.

"Yeah." He looked to the side. When he turned back, his gray eyes were intense and fixated on her. "About that." Sebastian blew out a noisy breath. "What the hell happened?"

Lola flinched at the feeling in his tone, suddenly wary. And confused.

"I mean...I don't understand." Even his voice was deeper. She didn't know this Sebastian.

She took another step back. "There's nothing to understand. You stopped talking to me last year. And now this year, for some reason, your guilty conscience has you sporadically trying to talk to me. And it's annoying."

The surprise on his face was palpable. "*I* stopped?" His voice rose. "*You* stopped talking to *me*, not the other way around." Anger laced his words and he stepped closer. "*You* stopped returning my phone calls, *you* were always busy when I stopped over, *you* avoided me. *You*, not me."

Fear reared up inside Lola, her breath leaving her in little panicked bursts. He was mad. Sebastian was upset and she didn't know him, didn't know this young man who used to be her friend. He could hurt her. He could hit her. Anyone could, if they were mad enough. She'd learned recently that you never truly knew someone until they showed their real self to you. She tripped over a limb and stumbled back, bumping into a tree as Sebastian advanced. She instinctively crouched down and covered her head, a whimper leaving her as she waited for the blow to come, only nothing happened.

Lola lowered her arm and looked up.

Sebastian stood there, brows furrowed. "What are you *doing?*"

She put a hand against the rough bark of the tree and got to her feet, feeling dumb. "Nothing. I fell."

He looked at the ground and then at her. "On what, a blade of grass?"

With a burning face, she said, "Yes. That's it."

It was past time for her to go—she'd embarrassed herself enough for the day. She started to walk away, wanting nothing more than to put large amounts of distance between her and Sebastian before she did something even more humiliating. Like crying. She was more than capable of doing that at this precise moment.

"So that's it, huh? You're just going to walk away?" he called after her.

She ignored him and picked up her pace.

"I never would have pegged you for a coward, Lola Murphy, but this last year has shown me the error of my ways," was his parting shot, and it stung.

All the way home his words ran through her head, overlapping, turning into a mantra until just one single word rang out, clear and unavoidable: coward. It wasn't true. None of it was true. He was a liar. *He'd* stopped talking to her. For no reason. And then Sebastian had the nerve to turn it around and act like it had been the other way around. Probably to make himself feel better. What had she possibly missed about him? He was overbearing, stubborn, and pushy.

And she was *not* a coward. Why did he even care if she was anyway? He had *Roxanne*. Lola shouldn't even enter his thoughts. Ever. She was sure she hardly ever did anyway. So it really shouldn't matter if she *was* a coward, not that she was. But if she was, what did it matter to him?

EVERY NIGHT FOR THE PAST two weeks when Lola got home from work, there he stood. This night was no different. He'd either somehow managed to find out her work schedule or he simply liked to stand outside in the cold and dark for whatever reason. She had a sneaky suspicion he had a hero complex and felt it was his duty to make sure she made it home from work okay. The irony of that did not escape her—she was pretty sure she was safer out on the streets than she was at home.

She wasn't in the mood for his charity, for his guilty conscience trying to make up for past snubs by looking out for her now. With the pale glow of streetlamps directing her to him, Lola strode across the street and toward Sebastian. The grass was stiff and crunched under her shoes. Even in the dark she could see his eyebrows lift as she approached. His hands were shoved in the pockets of his jacket, his breath leaving him in short spurts of frosty air.

Lola's nose and hands were cold, but the pull of her warm bed wasn't enough to keep her from confronting him. She stopped a few feet from him and looked up at him. His gray eyes met hers as he silently waited for her to speak.

"Stop it."

Sebastian cocked his head. "Stop what?"

"Stop...*this*." She waved a hand at him and her.

"Stop standing in my yard?"

"I don't need you looking out for me. I don't *want* you to. I'm *fine*. Always have been, always will be." Her throat tightened at the lie.

"I happen to like standing outside, and since it's my yard, I can."

She remembered his current look. He'd worn it when they'd argue, when he wouldn't admit to being wrong, when he made her do something she didn't want to do, but he somehow knew would be best for her. It was bullheaded and fierce—and she'd missed it.

"In the dark?"

"In the dark. And cold. And snow. And heat. Even in the rain." He leaned close and said, "Whenever I like."

Lola didn't know whether to laugh or get mad. Instead she made a sound of exasperation. "Fine. Whatever. Freeze. See if I care." She spun on her heel.

"Is everything okay?" he called after her.

Everything inside her froze, but she somehow managed to keep walking. "Yep. Everything's okay. Perfect. Wonderful. Super. Couldn't be better."

"I think you're lying."

That stopped her. No one had called her out before.

"At the park, you acted scared. Like you thought...like you thought I was going to *hit* you or something." His tone was incredulous, disbelieving.

She took a deep breath and clenched her hands into fists. She felt him move behind her, knew he stood close.

"What's going on with you? Whatever it is, you can talk to me. You know that."

If she leaned back, her back might even touch him. The heat of his breath fanned her hair and she shivered. She would give just about anything to feel his arms wrap around her, to feel safe, to have someone hug her, hold her. Lola sniffed and straightened her back.

"I want to help you. Let me help you."

She spun around and bumped into him, Sebastian's hands steadying her. He quickly dropped his hands and stepped back.

She swallowed and went on the offensive. "Why do you suddenly care?"

Sebastian blinked, opening his mouth. She didn't give him a chance to respond. Lola raced from him, away from her confusing thoughts and feelings. She didn't want to know what he had to say, what excuse or lie he would come up with. The fact was, he hadn't been there for her. He just couldn't suddenly start acting like he cared. Everything couldn't be okay with them. They couldn't go back. She couldn't forgive him.

LAST NIGHT SHE'D HEARD HIS footsteps pause outside her bedroom door. It made her sick just thinking about it. What reason had he had for stopping near her bedroom? She'd known it was him because of the heavier tread. He'd never bothered her during the night or while she was in her room before. Why hadn't he been at work? Lola hadn't been able to sleep the rest of the night. She'd been terrified he would open the door and—

"Miss Murphy."

She sat up and looked around the classroom. The walls had maps on them and a globe sat atop a bookshelf. It smelled of chalk in the room and someone's body odor. Lola was hot, but that had to be from nerves because it couldn't be over sixty-five in the room. Twenty-one pairs of eyes were on her, including the teacher's. Students snickered and her face heated up. Lola caught the eye of Roxanne and noted the smug look on her face. She was enjoying her embarrassment. Nothing new there.

Mr. Welsh was short, in his fifties, and had black curly hair. He was a hard teacher to get along with to begin with and anyone caught not paying attention usually regretted it. He always wore white dress shirts and khaki slacks. Some students, the braver, or stupider ones, depending on how you looked at it, joked that he only had one shirt and one pair of pants and had to do laundry every night.

"Yes?" she asked the history teacher.

Two bushy eyebrows lifted and he leaned his hips against the edge of his desk, crossing his arms. She felt her pulse pick up, knowing she was in for a chastising, and it wouldn't be a gentle one.

He didn't *do* gentle. His dark eyes drilled into hers. "What's the answer?"

She could tell by his expression he was enjoying her discomfort. Lola swallowed and looked at the blackboard for help, but it was blank. "Um…" Her palms turned sweaty and she turned to her classmates, but they were all conspicuously faced forward in their seats.

"Or maybe I should repeat the question?"

Her eyes flew to his and she nodded, relieved. "Yes. Please."

One corner of his thin mouth quirked up and he pushed away from the desk. "Of course, if you were *listening*, I wouldn't have to do that, now would I?" Mr. Welsh strode to the front of the room and faced the classroom. "Anyone want to help Miss Murphy out?"

Her heart pounded and that sick feeling from the night before returned, but for different reasons. No one said anything. Either they didn't know the answer, were scared to help her, or simply didn't want to.

He smiled and looked at Lola. "Since my class is so boring and unnecessary that you don't even pay attention, you might as well sit outside until it's over."

Her heartbeat tripped. "But—"

Mr. Welsh pointed at the door and said, "*Out.*"

Something snapped inside her. Rage, instant and red hot, swept through her. Trembling, she got to her feet and slammed her book on the desk. "No."

"What did you say?"

She seemed to have no control over the words leaving her mouth. "I didn't do anything wrong. I'm not leaving." Her voice and body quivered, tears threatened to fall, and her lips kept moving. "I don't deserve this." Her voice cracked.

The history teacher's lips thinned. "Now you have detention too. Go to the office. *Now.*"

The impulse to throw something was strong and her fingers tightened on her books. Mr. Welsh stared her down and she finally moved, avoiding the stunned eyes of her classmates and hurrying from the room.

Once outside, she leaned against a row of lockers and let her head drop back against the cool metal. Tears leaked from the corners of her eyes. What had she just done? What had she said? What was *wrong* with her? She didn't *do* things like that; she didn't have outbursts like that.

"Lola?" a small voice spoke.

A hand lightly touched her arm and she jerked away from the contact.

"Are you okay?" Concern pooled within the chocolate depths of Rachel Conrad's eyes.

They had once been close friends, but didn't talk much anymore outside of school. Rachel was one of those people who never had a bad thing to say about someone, who always saw the good in a person, even when it was hard to find. She was petite with short brown hair amd habitually wore black. Today was no different. She had on a black turtleneck and black slacks, the only splash of color being her blood red heels.

Lola glanced down at her plain purple long-sleeved tee, dark jeans, and tennis shoes. She felt underdressed next to her. Not that she had money to buy clothes like hers anyway. "What are you doing out here?"

Rachel had a loving mother and father, a younger brother and sister who looked up to her. She was praised instead of put down; she was hugged and told she was loved. She was *safe*. She couldn't understand what it was like to take every single breath with a hint of fear, to constantly be worrying about saying or doing the wrong thing, to always be watching for a blow to come, and yet never expecting it when it did.

"I volunteered to make sure you made it to the office, but really I just wanted to make sure you were okay."

She wanted to disappear, to vanish, to no longer be. "I'm fine." Lola turned toward the office.

"Lola."

She stopped, but didn't face her. "What?"

"Nothing. Never mind." Rachel's voice was tired.

She hesitated. They used to tell each other everything, just a year ago. She closed her eyes against a wave of tears. So much had changed. Lola had lost so much. She remembered the carefree, unimportant conversations they used to have that had been so vital to them. The giggles they'd shared. Their shopping adventures at the mall in the next city over. She missed all of that, but most of all she missed the illusion of safety she'd had.

Rachel's mother was a secretary at a law office; her father worked construction. They were by no means rich, but they were stable and happy. They had family meals and family game nights. They asked how everyone's day was and listened when one responded. Most importantly, they were *there*—and not just physically, but mentally, emotionally. They were on another planet from Lola and she had to remind herself that it would do her no good to try to think they had anything in common anymore. They didn't.

She gave herself a mental shake and went to the office.

LOLA SPENT DETENTION IN THE library, doodling on her notebook once her homework was finished. The room smelled musty and had pale wood paneling on the walls. There were five computers, lots of books, and Mrs. Horton. The librarian had to be in her seventies, but rumor had it she refused to retire. She wondered if eventually she'd just be kicked out of the school. She sat behind her desk, plump and red curly-haired, dressed in a black and pink floral print top and green slacks. She watched out of the corner of her eye as she shoved candy bars in her mouth and chewed away. Her stomach grumbled and Lola realized she hadn't eaten anything since the granola bar she'd choked down at lunch.

One other boy was in the room serving detention with her. He continually stared at her and she ignored him, but even though she avoided his eyes, she could *feel* them on her. He had shaggy black hair, pale green eyes, and a surly disposition. Lola couldn't remember his name, but she knew he was a senior like Sebastian and he got in trouble a lot. His jeans were always holey, his shirts black or red or some other dark color, and he liked to draw disturbing things. The boy was a loner, kept to himself. She didn't think he had many friends, if any. *A lot like you.*

"Time to go," Mrs. Horton announced at exactly five o'clock.

She packed her things up and shoved them in her backpack, intent on getting out of the school and away from the creepy boy as quickly as she could. Her footsteps echoed down the empty hallway. It was odd to be there afterhours and see the darkened, uninhabited rooms. It made her think of scary movies with predators lurking in dark corners and shadows. She shivered and picked up her pace.

"Hey. Goody Two Shoes."

Lola stumbled and glanced over her shoulder, unnerved to find the boy from detention not far behind. She hadn't even heard him.

"What did you call me?" She was immediately annoyed at the label and it showed in her voice. She was so *sick* of being ridiculed when she didn't deserve it.

One side of the boy's full mouth lifted and his eyes darkened, like he was having naughty thoughts about her. Lola's pulse tripped and she turned away. Ignoring him would probably be the best option.

Only he strode along beside her, looking completely at ease and in no hurry to go his own way. She glanced at him, surprised by how tall he was; he was even taller than Sebastian. He wasn't as muscular as Sebastian—his was a more lean build. He smelled faintly of cologne; expensive, good-smelling cologne.

Why am I even thinking of this? She pushed the door open, blinking in the blinding light of the sun. It was a nice day out, in the sixties with a light breeze. The wind caught her hair and played with it.

"I called you Goody Two Shoes. What were you in for? Did you forget to say please when you asked to go to the bathroom? Show up one minute late for class? Wear white on a red only day?"

Face on fire, she glared at him. He waited, an innocent look on his sharply angled face. "Are you enjoying yourself?"

"You have no idea," was his response.

"Well, I'm not. So…goodbye." She turned in the direction of her house, her steps leaden with dread.

"Lola." Softly spoken, like a caress.

She stopped and slowly turned to face the nameless boy, her breathing uneven. "Who *are* you?"

The sunlight hit him just right and he seemed to glow, become otherworldly, angelic even. She shook her head and he was just a troubled boy once more.

His lips twisted. "You don't remember me, do you?"

Something nagged at her subconscious, but she pushed it away, feeling sick. "No. I don't know you." *I don't want to know you.* Where had that come from?

An emotion flickered within the pale green depths of his eyes and was gone, his perpetual brood back in place. "The name's Jack, Goody Two Shoes. Jack Forrester."

"Don't *call* me Goody Two Shoes. It's not nice!"

He laughed. "It's not nice? Really? You can't even have a comeback that doesn't sound preppy."

Everyone was always ganging up on her, belittling her, criticizing her, making her feel less than. All that helplessness built up inside her and exploded. A burst of anger erupted in her and she reacted without thought. She slammed her palms against Jack's hard chest and shoved. It felt *amazing*. He propelled back, arms waving, and landed on his rear end in the grass with a grunt. His look of incomprehension was comical.

Lola put her hands over her mouth, eyes wide, and stared at him in horror. "Oh! I'm so sorry! I can't believe I just did that."

When Jack just sat there looking at her like he couldn't believe it either, laughter bubbled up. She was stunned by the sound of it, and her expression must have shown it, because Jack intently watched her, like he knew some secret about her even she didn't know.

Her laughter abruptly cut off. "Stop staring at me."

"I've never seen anyone look so surprised to be happy," he said quietly.

Her eyes burned and she swallowed. She grabbed her backpack she'd dropped at some point and raced home. She forced herself not to look back, not once. Why had he acted like she was supposed to know him, that she should remember him? Like they'd had some kind of interaction or shared some experience together. They never had. She would remember if they had. He was probably on drugs as well as being an academic failure and troublemaker. They all usually went hand and hand. Lola pushed the guilt she felt with that thought away and inwardly put a layer of armor on.

She was home.

CHAPTER 3

SHE CREPT PAST THE PARTIALLY opened bedroom door on the way to her own bedroom, hoping against hope that they were asleep and wouldn't know she was home two hours late from school. Supper would be late as well. Lola's stomach churned at the thought of possible repercussions. The floor creaked and gave her presence away. She went still, hoping they didn't hear, but when she heard the rustling of blankets, she knew it wasn't so.

"Lola, is that you?"

She closed her eyes. "Yes. I'm sorry for being noisy."

"Open the door."

She didn't want to open the door, she didn't want to see her mother and Bob in bed and think of the things they did there. It made her nauseous. How could her mother stand the look of him, the smell of him, his touch? Her mouth twisted at the thought of it.

"I have to get ready for work, Mom." That was a lie. She didn't have to work tonight—she just didn't want to be home either.

"Please come here." The weakness of her voice, the acute sorrow in it, pulled at Lola. She slowly pushed the door open. It smelled musty and unclean in the room. It smelled like Bob.

Her mother was huddled in the middle of the bed, looking small and child-like. A light blue blanket covered her and pillows propped her head up. The curtain was drawn, casting the room in shadows. With dizzying relief, she saw Bob wasn't in the room.

The room was small and sparse of furnishings. There was a bed and a dresser in the room, some framed photographs. Though Lola's room was small too, her mother had unselfishly given her the slightly larger one of the two. The walls were painted a pale green, which used to give her a sense of serenity, but now made her think of something sickly.

"Mom?" There was a catch to her voice, a waver in that one syllable word. She cleared her throat and made her way to the bed. She looked down at her mother, wondering at what precise moment their roles had reversed.

She kept hoping her mom would come back to her, that she'd suddenly wake up and be who she remembered her to be. Maybe the strong woman Lola remembered hadn't really ever been; maybe she was a figment of Lola's imagination. Why did she keep trying to catch a glimpse of that person? She supposed, on some level, she couldn't give up on her mom.

Lana patted the bed. "Sit down. I want to talk to you."

She silently shook her head. There was no way she would sit in the spot Bob slept, *no way*. She pretended not to see her mother's hurt look and instead focused on a framed photograph above the bed. It was a picture of her, taken when she was seven. Lola was missing her two front teeth and her eyes sparkled with happiness. Her skin had a healthy glow to it and she wore a purple dress with a red headband in her auburn hair. *Had I ever been so innocent?*

She turned away from the picture. "Where's Bob?"

Her mother folded over an edge of the blanket, her head down. "Out with friends."

'Out with friends' meant he was drinking at the bar. When he drank at the bar, he came home late and missed work. He also went from mean to really mean. All it took was a wrong look or word and he got scary real fast. Lola's stomach turned queasy and it was harder to take a breath.

"I thought...I thought maybe we could hang out tonight." Eyes full of hope fixed on Lola, waiting.

Her chest tightened. She wanted to. She so wanted her mother back, if only for one evening. She was *desperate* for her old mom. This new mom she didn't know and didn't like. Her lips parted and she almost said yes; was on the verge of it, but the urge to confront her mom was stronger. She had to try to get her mom to see reason.

"Mom, please leave him. We can leave tonight, while he's gone. We'll be okay without him, I promise. You'll be okay. *Please.*" Lola regretted the words as soon as she saw her mother's face.

Lana's face closed up and she retreated into herself.

She backed away, feeling sad even though she knew better than to. What was the point? She stopped near the door, pretending she hadn't just said that. "I can't hang out tonight. I have to work. Remember?"

Her eyes dropped, and another little sliver of life seemed to slip from her, dimming her. "Oh. That's right. I thought you had Thursdays off usually."

I do. Lola closed her eyes, torn with needing her mother and never wanting to see this version of her again, even if this was the only part of her that there would ever be again. *I want you back, Mom, I want you back. But you're not her anymore. I don't know you.*

She took a deep breath and opened her eyes. "I'm sorry, Mom."

I'm sorry our lives are the way they are. I'm sorry you're not strong enough. I'm sorry you don't love me enough. I'm sorry I'm not enough for you. Lola walked out the door, wanting to escape her mother's pain and sadness, wanting to escape the house, Bob, her life. Her mother's disappointment was like a heavy weight in the air and it was stifling.

She couldn't stay there, she couldn't be there. Part of her wanted to leave, to run away and never return. Some fledgling sense of loyalty wouldn't allow her to leave her mother, but that didn't mean she wanted to be around her either. It hurt too much. And she was so angry with her. She hated what she had become almost as much as she hated Bob.

THE OUTSIDE AIR WAS REFRESHING after the stale interior of the house. The sun was lowering in the sky, turning the horizon into pretty shades of pink and orange. Images of her mother haunted Lola as she walked down the streets of Morgan Creek. The tinkle of her laughter, the sparkle in her blue eyes. The way she used to hold Lola close and whisper that she loved her.

She almost turned back. She yearned to rush into her mother's arms and be held. To hold her mother like she used to. She couldn't. Her mother was tainted by Bob's touch and scent. It wasn't *her* anymore. She had to keep reminding herself of that. Tears flowed down her cheeks, warm against her cool flesh.

Not for the first time she ached for her father. Joe Murphy had died of cancer when he was twenty-eight and she was four. All he was to her was a photograph of a young man whose chin and nose she'd inherited; someone whose memory her mother's eyes and voice softened over—a ghost of a person almost completely faded from her mind. Someone, who if he still lived, would have made Lola's life so very different from the way it was.

There was a longing within her for a father she would never know, and Bob being his replacement made it all that much more unbearable. From what her mother had told her, he'd been a good man, but she didn't trust her mother's definition of what a good man was, not anymore. But she liked to believe he had been. She liked to believe he'd loved her and never would have hurt her. What few pictures she'd seen of her father told her he had. Lola could take some comfort from that.

She found herself at the creek the town was named after. It ran through the middle of Morgan Creek and met up with the Mississippi River at some point. Children liked to fish in it. There was a cemented path on the side of it people walked or rode bikes on. She stared into the gray water and listened to the sound of it lapping against rocks as the current pulled it downstream. Her eyes closed as she held herself still, a sense of peace slowly encompassing her. She took a deep breath and slowly let it out.

Lola had one more year of school to get through and then she could leave the house that was no longer a home. She wished she could leave as soon as she turned eighteen in September, but where would she go? She had no other relatives. At least none her mother talked to. She vaguely remembered an aunt—her father's sister. She didn't know anything about her and her mother never brought her up. She sensed something had happened between the two of them and that was why she was just a faceless being she didn't know. There was no one, and even if there was, she wouldn't want to burden them with the responsibility of having to take care of her.

A familiar, cruel snicker sounded behind her. Lola stiffened, but didn't move, hoping she would just pass by. Of course that was wishful thinking.

"Well, well, well, looky here. It's the detention queen," a singsong voice called.

She slowly faced Roxanne. "What do you want?" She didn't understand why she continued to pick on her for whatever reason. This unjustified bullying seemed so trite compared to what she faced every day at home. It was childish and petty.

She tossed her head and placed a hand on a hip. A green hooded sweatshirt emphasized her eyes and dark skinny jeans molded to her legs. "What do I want? Let's see." She tapped her cheek and cocked her head. Almost immediately Roxanne straightened as her eyes narrowed. "I want you to stay away from my boyfriend."

She took a step back in surprise at the look of loathing on Roxanne's face. Even her cold beauty was blocked out by it, leaving something ugly in its place. "That's not a problem."

"Yeah. I almost believe that. Except I know Sebastian has been waiting outside his house every night to make sure you get home okay from work. I don't like it."

Lola knew it would do no good to explain that she didn't know why he was doing that, nor did she *want* him to do that. "How do you know that?"

Roxanne took a step closer. "Because he *told* me. Says he feels *bad* for you, like there might be something wrong at your house." She stopped. "Sebastian has a big heart and thinks he needs to protect people."

She knew better than anyone just how big his heart was and how protective he could be. Resentment that his girlfriend knew as well reared up, but Lola squashed it down. Roxanne was his girlfriend, of *course* she knew things like that. She *should* know things like that. Lola had merely been his friend—nothing more—since she'd moved in across the street thirteen years ago. She wasn't anymore. She had to remember that.

"I know. You should tell him to quit that."

Roxanne's lips thinned. "I don't know what game you're playing at, but you might as well stop."

"Game? I have no idea what you're talking about."

"This past year you've lost weight, gotten all pale, and have this sad look on your face all the time. You don't talk to anyone. You've turned *creepy*." Her hands fisted at her sides. "And now you try to be cool by getting in trouble. You obviously want attention."

Lola was stunned by her words, by the heat in her tone. Was that what people thought? That she had withdrawn and changed as a ploy to get attention? Bitter anger swept through her. "You don't know…what you're talking about," she choked out, close to tears.

She laughed. "I know you want Sebastian back in your life and I know it's not going to happen." Her nostrils flared as she leaned toward Lola. "You stay away from my boyfriend. *Or else.*"

Her skin burned. "Or else *what?*"

She jabbed a long fingernail at Lola, piercing the sensitive skin below her neck. "Or else you'll be sorry. I mean it. Stay away from him." Roxanne flounced past, taking the scent of raspberries and loathing with her.

She raised a shaking hand to her neck and touched the sore spot. Roxanne wasn't just nasty, as she'd first thought; she was *scary*. Sick with all that had happened in recent days, Lola fell to a bench and let it hold her up.

What Roxanne said were lies. Regardless of whether it was true or not, it still hurt. And telling her to stay away from Sebastian when he'd barely spoken to her in a year? That wouldn't be hard to do. Her life was such a mess. She felt so helpless, like everyone else controlled her with their actions and words.

I wonder what would happen if I wasn't here anymore? The forbidden thought scared her—that she would think such a thing and that Lola wondered if it really mattered if she was around or not.

IT WAS DARK BY THE time she got home—cold enough out that she could see her breath in the air. Lola timed it so that it was around the time she usually got home from work. She'd even worn her work clothes so there was no suspicion. She supposed if Bob had decided to check up on her at work it wouldn't have mattered what she was wearing when she got home.

Before she made it to the front door she heard something smash against a wall.

Bob swore.

Lana softly cried.

Lola's pulse raced.

She couldn't go in there. Anytime he was mad, it was somehow her fault. She quietly backed away from the door, eyes trained on it. He never hit her mother, but his words were often cruel. She should be okay for now, and with her leaving for work soon, she didn't have to be around him much longer. But then it would be just the two of them, and that realization made her stomach clench.

Lola wordlessly shook her head, stumbling over a tree root and catching herself before she could fall. She turned and stared at Sebastian's house, imagining the scene inside was much more peaceful and calm than the one that awaited her. Lights shone through the windows and the television was on in the living room; the house and those within it beckoning to her.

She ducked her head against the chilly breeze and hurried down the street. It would be worse for her to show up later, but maybe Bob would be passed out, and whatever he would do would have to wait until the next day. It would be one less day of abuse to endure. She knew her rationalizing didn't make sense, but right now, to her, it did. Daytime monsters weren't as scary as nighttime ones, no matter what he did to her.

A car drove by, and for one terrifying second, Lola thought it was Bob coming to get her, but the vehicle passed without slowing. She exhaled deeply and went down an alley, deciding to stay off the main streets. Her light jacket wasn't doing much against the cold and she shivered, wishing she had a warmer one.

When a cat yowled, she jumped, her eyes constantly scanning the dark for a possible unknown predator. She kept walking until she was near a wooded area on the outskirts of town, only stopping then. A forest of trees surrounded her, looking ominous in the dark, but somehow familiar too. Had she been there before? She didn't think so.

A limb cracked under her shoes as she made her way to a rock slab big enough to sit on. Or hide under. It sat high and jutted out, like an upside down L. When a shadow moved, her pulse picked up.

"Wondered how long it would take you to show up again." The voice came from the far side of the rock, low and mocking.

"Who's there?" she demanded, her heart pounding. She had the insane thought Bob had somehow gotten there before her and lay in wait for her. Impossible, but fear was rarely logical.

The shadow moved and a form jumped to the ground. It lengthened and shaped into a young man. He was clothed in black, making it difficult to see him in the night. Lola thought maybe that was the point. He smoothed long bangs back from his forehead and strode toward her. His green eyes caught her attention first, then his lowered eyebrows. "Well, I'm *not* your knight in shining armor. I'll leave that title to Sebastian Jones."

His words confused her, along with the way he said them. What did he mean by that? "What are you doing here?"

Jack leaned against a tree and crossed his arms. "I could ask you the same thing. I'm always here. This is where I come when I can't handle life." He craned his head back and looked at the sky. His lips curved sardonically and he glanced at her. "Which is why I'm here just about every night."

His unshielded honesty tugged at her. Lola could relate to that. How many times in a single day did she wish she could escape her life? She took a step closer as she asked, "Why are you in trouble all the time?" She looked at the twinkling stars as she waited for him to answer. He smelled like laundry detergent, his cologne from earlier now faded. The scent of clean clothes was just as appealing as the cologne had been—a thought that made her face heat up.

"Why were you in detention today?"

She was unnerved to find his gaze locked on her. She shoved her hands in her jacket pockets and looked away. "Mr. Welsh was picking on me."

"He picks on *everyone*. Why take it personally?"

"I don't know," she answered. It did seem silly now. She'd just been so fed up, so angry, so tired of never standing up for herself.

"I'm in detention all the time because I don't want to go home. Can't go home if I have detention, right?"

She sucked in a sharp breath and glanced at him. "What happens at home?"

Jack's lips pressed together and he shrugged. "Dad likes to knock me around. He works from six at night until six in the morning. If I'm lucky he's gone by the time I get home."

Suddenly she saw Jack Forrester in a whole new light. He wasn't a druggie, a troublemaker, or an academic failure. He was an abused boy trying to deal with it the only way he knew how. He was *her*. Lola felt sick, like she couldn't breathe. She backed away from him, staring into knowing eyes.

"What's your excuse, Goody Two Shoes?"

A breeze picked up Jack's shaggy hair and blew it across his eyes. The lower part of his face was visible, slivers of his eyes glowing through strands of hair. It was unsettling.

She licked dry lips and asked a question of her own. "Do you ever...do you ever fight back?"

He stiffened, turning away as he nodded. "Oh yeah, all the time. But then he goes after my sister instead." He swung around to face her, locking her in place with the intensity of his eyes. "*Once*. Once I fought back. Bastard hit my sister so hard she couldn't see out of her left eye for a week. He just needs a punching bag." He spread his arms wide. "I'm it."

She pressed her arm against her midsection and swallowed with difficulty. "I'm so sorry."

How could he stand it, *years* of it? Bob had been around for one and that was close to unbearable. Jack had probably been abused his whole life. He had to be eighteen, or close to it. If he wasn't failing his classes, he would graduate in a little over a month. He could *leave*. And why was he telling her all of this, someone he'd never spoken to before today? She was a stranger, really.

"Don't be sorry." He moved away, pulled himself onto the rock, and offered her a hand.

She hesitated, and then put her hand within his warm, calloused one. He lifted her easily and released her hand once she was on the rock. For that brief instant their hands touched, she'd felt a connection to another human being. When was the last time she'd had that? Her mother kept her distance physically as well as mentally, but even if she tried to comfort her, Lola didn't know if she'd let her now.

"How do you stand it?"

He shrugged, looking away. "I just deal with it, do what I got to do. Stay invisible as much as possible. I'm an adult. I could leave. I don't for my sister. You know her?" Jack tilted his head as he studied her. "No. You wouldn't, would you? She would be beneath your notice."

She glared at him and scooted away to put more distance between them. "I don't know why you act like I'm some kind of snob. I'm not. Never have been."

"Not this year."

She drew her knees to her chest and wrapped her arms around them. People and their assumptions—none of them right. *What did you assume about Jack?* her conscience chimed in, and she made a face. "You don't even know me," she reminded him.

He paused. "Right. Anyway, she's a sophomore. Pretty little blonde with big brown eyes." She scrutinized his face and hair, noting how dissimiliar that was to him. He caught her look and laughed. "Yeah. She looks nothing like me, lucky kid. She loves to sing and she has the sweetest voice."

She was shocked by the depth of feeling she heard in his voice. She wouldn't have thought him capable of such emotion. One more assumption she would have gotten wrong. She'd told him he didn't know her. But she also didn't know him.

"What's her name?"

"Isabelle."

She made a mental note to find out who Isabelle Forrester was. "What exactly was I like last year? According to *you*, that is."

"You may."

"But you won't answer?"

"I can answer. I just don't know if you want to hear it."

"Go ahead."

He glanced at her, one side of his mouth lifted. His eyes gleamed in the dark. "Okay. You thought you were above others."

Anger shot through her. "I never—"

"What do you think I'm like?" he interrupted.

She ground her teeth together. "I don't know what you're talking about."

"Oh, come on. Yes, you do. Tell me. I'm waiting," he added when she said nothing.

"I don't know anything about you," she insisted.

"But you thought you did, earlier," he pressed. "I could tell by the look on your face."

She shifted, uncomfortable with that observation. "Okay, fine. I thought things and I was wrong. Same as you. But I never thought I was better than anyone."

"Sure, Goody Two Shoes," he mocked quietly.

"I wish you wouldn't call me that." Frustrated, she turned her head away, staring into the night. If she had ever acted like that, she was sorry, but she just didn't see it. She didn't remember ever putting anyone down or going out of her way to make others feel inferior. If that was the way Jack had chosen to believe she was, then that was too bad.

"So, *Lola*, what do you like to do?"

It was such an unoriginal, *normal* question she gave a surprised laugh. Twice in one day, and both in Jack's presence. Strange.

"What do I like to do?" What did she like to do anymore? Last year that question would have had lots of answers: shopping, dancing, watching movies, hanging out with her friends.

This year she had one answer. "I like to write."

He eyed her. "Really?"

"Yes, *really*. Why is that so hard to believe?"

"What, like, sappy love stories?"

She felt her face heat up. "*No*. Like, poems, and stuff." She waited for his laughter. It never came.

"Can I read one sometime?"

She froze. No one had ever asked to read her work; no one ever *had* read her work. She didn't even know if anyone knew she liked to write. Although...someone did now—Jack. She looked at him. "If I can see one of your drawings."

It was his turn to go still. "Uh..."

Lola nudged his shoulder. "Fair is fair."

After a moment, he blew out a breath. "Okay."

"But it can't be one of those creepy ones you always draw."

One side of his mouth quirked up. "Example?"

She shifted, the rock digging into her sensitive flesh. "You know, like demons and zombies and whatever else you draw at school."

"You're a fan, are you?"

"Not exactly."

"Yet you know my work. Must be a fan."

"Whatever."

"Whatever is the comeback one uses when one does not have a proper comeback."

"Whatever," she said again, slightly smiling.

He leaned back and propped his head up with his arms. Lola did the same. They watched the stars and and tree limbs sway with the wind. It was a comfortable quiet and she felt more at ease than she had in months. She didn't understand why she was able to feel comfortable around a mouthy stranger who didn't have the best opinion of her, or why she was telling him things she'd never told anyone else—maybe it was *because* she didn't know him that she was able to open up to him.

Whatever it was, she was thankful for it. She didn't have to pretend everything was okay around Jack; she didn't have to be on guard. She could just...*be*. Although he'd never asked about her life at home, she still felt like he knew, and accepted, and didn't judge.

"You can come here whenever you need to. I'll be here," he said after a long silence.

Those words warmed her. She didn't say anything, but a small smile took hold of her lips. She didn't feel so alone anymore.

CHAPTER 4

LOLA BOLTED UPRIGHT IN HER bed, some internal clock of hers telling her she'd overslept. Her eyes shot to the clock and she moaned at the red numbers glaring back at her. She rushed around the room, throwing on a blue shirt and jeans, followed by quickly brushing the snarls from her hair and tackling her teeth with a toothbrush and toothpaste.

She paced outside her mother's bedroom door, gnawing on her thumbnail. If she didn't get a ride, she would be late. She had her driver's license, but there was only one vehicle and it was Bob's. No way would he let her take it. Lola couldn't believe the luck she'd had last night. She'd heard Bob snoring away in the bedroom when she'd gotten home after midnight. Now, because of her sleeping late, she was going to stir the beast before the beast was ready to stir, which would make it so much worse.

You should have known. This is what you get for thinking you could outsmart him, even one time. You should have just gone inside instead of taking off.

She chewed her lip as she stared at the cracked white paint of the door. There was one rule she knew better than to break: never disturb them when the door was closed. But she couldn't afford another detention the very next day after getting her first ever. She swallowed and hesitantly knocked on the door. There was no response so she knocked again.

She heard Bob curse right before the door was flung open. He glared at her, his eyes squinty and red. His thin hair stuck up in tufts and he had on a pair of boxers. Lola instinctively recoiled from the sight and smell of him. "What?" he snapped, hands gripping either side of the door frame.

"I...I overslept and..." She gestured with her hands, avoiding his gaze. "I'm going to be late if I don't get a ride. Can I please get a ride to school?" she whispered.

Bob moved so fast she had no time to react. He shoved her into the hallway. "You little moron! Can't even get your ass to school on time. God *damn* it!"

Lola stumbled and fell against the wall. "I'm sorry," she got out through lips numb with fear.

Spittle flew from his mouth as he yelled, "You're gonna be sorry!"

She flinched back, but she wasn't fast enough. The crack of his hand against her face jerked her head to the side. She fell against the wall and put a hand to her face, the coolness of her palm at odds with the burning flesh. Her breath left her in short gasps and she stared at the brown carpet, her body trembling. She stayed like that, waiting for whatever was next to come.

"Get your ass to the car." He kicked the door open wider and went inside the bedroom.

She briefly closed her eyes, fighting not to cry. She grabbed her backpack from the floor and walked. She didn't look into the bedroom, didn't check to see if her mother was awake or whether she had witnessed what had just happened. She was sure she had.

She hurried down the hallway with her head lowered, hot tears streaming down her cheeks. Lola carefully shut the front door behind her, the cool air stinging her already tender flesh. She forced her legs to keep moving though they wanted nothing more than to collapse beneath her. Her hands shook and she didn't get the black Buick's door open until the second try. She gingerly sat on the dirty seat. Fast food wrappers and soda cans crumpled under her feet. It smelled like body odor in the car and she put a hand over her nose and mouth.

As she sat waiting, a low moan escaped her. It sounded like a wounded animal and she was stunned that such a noise could come from her. Her face hurt, but inside was what hurt the most. Helplessness cocooned her. Lola felt so lost. She wrapped her arms around her midsection and let the sobs overtake her. Footsteps reached her ears and she quickly wiped her eyes, being careful around her sore eye and cheek.

Bob, dressed in a blue shirt with holes, red and black plaid pajama pants, and snow boots, climbed into the vehicle. He didn't look at her, didn't say a word. She pressed her body against the door, trying to get as much space between them as possible without him noticing. The ride was minutes long, but seemed to take hours. She jumped from the car as soon as he pulled up to the curb of the school, hurrying up the steps that led to Morgan Creek High, careful not to look at anyone.

Rachel waved at her from her locker. She had on a short jean skirt and a black blazer with knee-high boots. Her short brown hair was a disarrayed mess that looked fashionable. She waved back, but kept walking. She didn't want to talk to anyone, especially not Rachel with her never-ending supply of good intentions.

She unlocked her locker, shoved her backpack inside, and headed for the art room.

"Lola! Wait up." She fell into step beside her, offering a bright smile. "How was detention? Mr. Welsh is such a jerk."

"It wasn't so bad." An image of Jack's mocking smile floated through her head. She felt something weird in the pit of her stomach and shook her head.

"I'm glad you survived." Rachel offered a smile she didn't return. "So, uh, I was wondering if you wanted to hang out this weekend? My family is going to some dumb movie Saturday night I refuse to go to. We haven't hung out forever. A sleepover would be fun. What do you think? Want to?" She spoke quickly, her words jumbling together in what seemed like nervousness.

Lola looked at her, surprised by the invitation. They hadn't interacted outside of school for so long she'd assumed they wouldn't be again. Rachel looked so hopeful that she felt herself weakening. Maybe she could have a night with no worries, maybe she could forget for a while.

You can't. Remember this morning.

Rachel leaned closer, her eyes widening. "What happened to your face?"

Her pulse picked up and she averted her face, beginning to walk again. "Nothing." *Go away, Rachel, go away and don't wonder.*

She caught up to Lola, concern lowering her brows. "It just looks...swollen or something. Are you sure it's nothing?"

"Yep. I have to go to the bathroom. I'll see you in class," she said in a rush, veering toward the bathrooms and away from Rachel.

She was relieved to find the pink restroom empty, letting out a sigh when it became apparent she wasn't being followed. The room smelled like soap and paper towels. She rushed to the mirror and stared at her reflection. Her bones were so prominent they were almost skeletal. Lola flinched at the realization, wondering why she hadn't noticed how bad it was getting. She needed to eat more. *Hard to do when almost everything comes right back up.*

She turned her head to the side, examing her latest battle wound. The flesh near the corner of her right eye was pink and puffy with an angry welt. Lola leaned closer, dismayed to find a small purple bruise already forming. "Great," she mumbled.

Fighting tears, she leaned against the sink, wanting this to be over with. Some days she could accept that she had close to a year left to get through before it would get better. Other days, like today, she didn't know if she could do it. She just wanted him *gone*. But even if he *was* gone, what would that mean for her and her mother? She didn't know how things could ever be normal between them again, or if they be any variation of how they used to be.

She didn't know if she could forgive her mother for the year of hell she'd subjected her to. Especially when she didn't even seem to *care*. The mother she knew and loved wasn't there anymore and Lola didn't know if she would ever come back. A cry of frustration and anger and pain erupted from her. She glared at her reflection, hating what she saw, hating what she had become. The past year had changed both her and her mother. She gripped the sink so hard her knuckles turned white. She closed her eyes and took deep breaths. *Get a grip. Don't lose it.*

Lola turned the water on and splashed some on her face, hoping it would take some of the swelling away. The bruise she could do nothing about. She arranged her long hair so that it partially covered the right side of her face. It was the best she could do.

When she left the bathroom, it was to find the hallway already empty and that first period had started. She was late anyway. *All that for nothing.*

Art was one of her favorite classes. There were fifteen kids in the classroom, all busy on their projects. They talked and laughed to one another, their biggest concern what they would be doing that night after school. Lola had been like them too, just last year. She inhaled the scent of paint as she went to her easel, hoping the teacher, Mr. Roberts, wouldn't notice she hadn't been there when the bell sounded. No such luck. He immediately made his way to her.

"Miss Murphy. You're late." He was a big, towering man with white hair and glasses. His voice boomed throughout the room and conversations halted.

Her face burned. *Great. I'm sure I'll get another detention.* She looked at the outline of a butterfly on the 8 X 10 canvas, keeping her face curtained by her hair. "I'm sorry."

Mr. Roberts paused. "Is everything okay?"

Her breath hiccupped and it took her a moment to find her voice. "Yes. Everything's fine."

"Okay then. Get to work." He moved away and voices picked up where they'd left off.

She looked down at her tennis shoes. *No one cares.* She pushed her hair behind her ears and stared at her unfinished art project, not sure where to begin. Usually able to lose herself in her painting, Lola felt uninspired and emotionless.

"Look at her. She doesn't even realize she only put eye shadow on *one* eye." Snickers followed Roxanne's words. She seemed to be the biggest target of her malice and yet it didn't immediately register with her that of course Roxanne was talking about her.

Lola frowned. *I didn't put eye shadow on* any *eye.*

"Maybe I should give her some makeup pointers." More laughter and a couple girls chimed in that they would help.

She sucked in a breath and quickly blanketed her face with her hair, wanting to disappear. Roxanne had to be talking about the small purple bruise above her right eye. She kept her face forward and hoped her antagonizer would lose interest in her if she didn't respond.

"Shut up, Roxanne. Like anyone would want makeup tips from *you.*" There was stunned silence after that because *no one* said things like that to Roxanne Zanders.

Lola looked behind her and caught Rachel's eye. Rachel smiled. Gratitude trickled through her, easing some of the discord within her, and she turned back to her art project. As she stared at it, she chewed on her lower lip and let inspiration wash over her. She let it encompass her and the outline of a butterfly turned into four black, bold letters. Slashes of color made up the background and became interwoven with the letters. She set the paintbrush down, looking at what she had created.

When the bell rang, Roxanne sprang to her feet and strode from the room with her posse in tow, but not before giving Rachel and Lola her signature glare.

"You just got an enemy," she said as they walked down the hallway. Kids bustled past on either side of them, loud and full of energy. Her eyes unconsciously searched the crowded hallway for a distinct form. She told herself it wasn't disappointment she felt when she didn't find him. One or two conversations and a similar home life did not make them anything.

Rachel shrugged. "I'd rather have her for an enemy than a friend. Can you imagine? Dressing and talking like *that* to fit in, not having a mind of my own, *no* thank *you*. Besides, I'm sick of her picking on you. You should be too. She only does it because she's jealous of you."

"Right." Why would Roxanne have any reason to be envious of her? She was pretty, popular, had a good body, and all the boys drooled after her. No, that wasn't it. She was just mean.

As she watched, Roxanne stopped at Sebastian's locker. He had on a dark blue shirt and faded jeans, looking strong, steady—looking like her safety blanket just out of reach. Yearning for her friend stamped itself on her heart, painfully squeezing it. Roxanne tapped him on the shoulder and he looked up, a smile lighting up his face at the sight of her.

Lola's stomach knotted and she looked away. She didn't understand why it was still hard to see him, but it was. Probably because she didn't know what had happened between them that had made them the way they were. And of course part of her missed him—really, all of her missed him. They'd grown up together. He'd been her first, longest, and best friend.

Rachel pointed at Sebastian. "*That*, right there, is why she doesn't like you."

She hurried past them with her head down. "That doesn't make any sense. We don't even talk anymore."

"Yeah. What's up with that anyway?" She leaned against the lockers as Lola unlocked hers and grabbed books for her next class.

She slammed her locker door shut. "Nothing."

Rachel put a hand on her arm when she tried to turn away, forcing her to look at her. "Us too. We barely talk anymore. What happened?"

"I'm just...busy."

The grip tightened on her arm. "And your face?"

Lola glanced at her friend's determined features. "What about my face?"

"Pretty sure that isn't purple makeup. Who did that to you? Was it your mom's husband?"

She swallowed. She desperately wanted to tell someone, to tell Rachel. But what would happen then? She would look at her in horror—probably never speak to her again. Or she'd tell a teacher and Lola would have to talk to them, maybe someone would even call the authorities. Then what? Then nothing would happen. Or maybe she'd be taken from her mother. But most likely it would do no good and she'd be even more alienated than she already was from the kids her age and Bob would just get worse.

The bell buzzed and she wrenched her arm from Rachel's grasp, ignoring her as she called her name. She rushed down the corridor to Geometry with a pounding heart. She couldn't tell anyone.

CHAPTER 5

LOLA THOUGHT SHE MIGHT GET sick, but she kept walking. Trying not to hurry, trying not to run, she made her way out into the sunlit day. She didn't want to draw attention to herself, but she also wanted to get away from the school as quickly as possible. She strode down the steps of the school, intent on putting distance between herself and the building before someone noticed her absence.

The sun was warm on her head and Lola shook off her jacket, shoving it into her backpack as she walked. Old structures boasted of the town's history and age. Leafy green trees were abundant and the scent of lilacs was heady. Visually, it was a beautiful town. Instead of heading into the main part of town, she went toward the edge of it, toward the wooded part.

Every car that drove by caused her heartbeat to escalate, but none of them stopped. Lola wouldn't meet the eyes of people she passed on the sidewalk. It seemed to take forever to get to her destination, but really it was less than ten minutes. She wondered what she was doing. Lola had never skipped school before. It was like some reckless being was shoving itself to the surface and taking over her She felt different from who she was now, but nothing like who she used to be.

She wondered if Jack would be there. She hadn't seen him anywhere at school. She wondered if his father had hurt him, making it impossible for him to be at school, and the thought caused her throat to tighten. With grass and dirt beneath her feet, and trees all around her, Lola stopped at the clearing. She felt him before she saw him. The air brought the scent of his cologne to her like a caress of hello, but the rock, pale gray and jagged, held no figure. She turned in a circle, trying to catch a glimpse of the boy.

"Lola."

She whirled around, hair clinging to her lips. She pushed the strands away, holding still as he approached. Jack made his way around the rock and toward her. He had on ripped jeans and a white tee shirt with unlaced black boots on his feet. Locks of black hair fell over his forehead and his upper lip curled in its derisive way.

"Miss me?"

When he was a few short feet away she saw the cut in his lip, the bloody slit scabbing over on his left cheekbone. She closed her eyes, feeling sick. A cool, light touch on her right eye had her stiffening. She opened her eyes to see the tightening around Jack's, the way his lips pressed into a thin line. Their eyes met for one charged moment and his hand dropped.

"What a dynamic duo we make, huh?" he said, turning away.

"Like Batman and Robin?"

He glanced at her, a small smile on his lips. "Exactly like that. I'm Batman."

"Sure. Whatever. You can be Batman." She paused. "What happened?" Her voice sounded rough and unused as she asked the question.

He hopped onto the rock like an agile mountain lion. He crouched there, looking straight ahead. The muscles in his arms and legs were taut and her body responded, perplexing her. She wasn't attracted to him. Or at least, she didn't think she was. She *shouldn't* be. Not that he wasn't handsome, he was. But his features were hard, cynical, angular, *cold*. Jack Forrester did *not* have a sunny disposition. He was nothing like what she had ever thought she'd be attracted to.

"What's your favorite kind of food?"

She blinked and looked away from his sinewy form. "I don't know."

"Come on. Everyone's got one favorite meal. If you had to pick one thing to eat every meal, every day, for the rest of your life, what would it be?"

What a silly question.

She didn't eat much because of her stomach always being upset. Lola used to enjoy food. Maybe a little too much. Chocolate cake with chocolate frosting, chocolate chip cookies, French fries, hamburgers, pizza—her mouth watered.

"Pizza," she answered definitively.

Jack shot her a look. "Pizza?"

"Yes. Pizza. You get all your food groups too. Cheese, meat, veggies, fruit, grain." She shrugged. "Whatever."

"That's weak, Lola, *weak*. Is whatever your favorite word?"

"It might be. What's your favorite? Something manly like steak and potatoes?"

Jack cocked his head, appearing to give the question a lot of thought. His lips twitched as he answered, "Actually, I like pizza too. But it has to be all meat. Vegetables aren't allowed on my pizza."

They shared a smile and her stomach flip-flopped. She leaned against the rock so her gaze wouldn't keep going to him. "How come you weren't in school today? Because of your face?"

"How come you skipped out? Because of your face?" he tossed back. He jumped to the ground beside her, startling her. "Come on. Let's go for a walk."

She stared at his offered long-fingered hand. Lola didn't understand how she could breathe easier just by being near him, or why her current world seemed a distant, old memory. She was untouchable by her reality while in his presence. Maybe it was because there was no fear of judgment, of seeing pity and horror in his eyes. Maybe it was because they were going through the same thing. He didn't need her to talk about it because he understood. In fact, he seemed to want the exact opposite—to pretend there wasn't any terrible thing *to* talk about.

She grabbed his hand and held it tight. Did she imagine he lightly squeezed it before releasing it?

They didn't look at each other as they walked over fallen limbs and loose rocks, brittle twigs snapping under their shoes. The sun filtered through the many high branches, a kaleidoscope of heat and light flickering over them. It was silent except for the chatter of small animals and the chirping of birds.

"Favorite band?"

She started at the sound of his deep voice. "Uh...P!nk?"

"Are you asking or telling?"

"P!nk," she said firmly.

"Why P!nk?"

"Because she's strong, mentally and physically. She's tough and she doesn't take crap from anyone. Her music can be light or it can be deep. There's the pop side to her and the one that makes you feel something when you listen to her music. It's like there are two sides to her, just like everyone. She's complicated and diverse and phenomenal. Plus she's a great dancer."

"What?" she demanded when she noticed he was staring at her.

"Nothing. Just...that's a really in depth description."

"Sorry." She felt her skin heat up.

"No. It's…I like it. And stop apologizing. You don't need to be sorry for talking to me. I won't even hold it against you if you want to talk a lot."

Her eyes flew to his. She caught his smile and was warmed by it. "How about you?"

"That's easy. Muse."

"Why?"

"They're kick ass."

After her lengthy narrative, Jack's three words made her laugh. He laughed too and her flesh tingled at the rumbling sound. He had a nice laugh.

"How's Granger's?"

She glanced at him, surprised he knew she worked there. "It's a job. I work and make money." She shrugged. "Do you work anywhere?"

"Yeah." One corner of his mouth lifted in a cynical smirk. "I help out on Jared Summers' farm. Know him?" When she shook her head, he continued, "He lives down the road from us. He's a quiet guy, decent."

"Have you worked there long?"

He gave a short bark of laughter. "Yeah. Since I was twelve. At least, that's when I started hanging out there, pestering him. Every day I walked over to his farm, asking for something to do, practically begging to be put to work—anything to get away from my dad. I did what I could, but I think I got in his way more than anything. Jared didn't have the heart to tell me to go home. He acts tough, but he's really not. I think he knew I needed to be there, needed somewhere to go. When I got old enough, he put me to work."

"Do you like it?" She didn't know anything about farming, nor did she particularly want to.

It was his turn to shrug. "Helps buy groceries."

Her brows furrowed. Jack made her re-evaluate her situation fast. People had it worse than her; him being one of those people. She knew he would hate her pity just as she would hate his, but she felt so bad for him, for his life that wasn't really a life. She wondered how long he'd had the role of brother *and* father to his younger sister.

They were silent after that.

Jack was so much taller than she was; her head was barely at level with his shoulder. The sides of their bodies grazed one another as they made their way through the woods. She couldn't believe how comfortable she felt around a boy she barely knew. It was like they were kindred spirits in misfortune. No words were necessary. Twigs snapped under the weight of their shoes. Squirrels scampered around them, keeping their distance. And the birds sang breathtakingly beautiful songs. It was exactly what she needed.

"What do you want to do after school's finished?" he asked, his quiet voice breaking the stillness.

Live, was the first thought that popped into her head. She stopped walking, frowning at the truth of it. "I don't know," was all she said.

"Liar," he said softly.

Her face heated up. She didn't consider herself a liar—there were simply some things she didn't want to tell people, and so she evaded answering certain questions. "I want to go to college."

"For?"

She reached down and picked up a twig. She snapped it into little pieces. "I don't know for sure, something with writing." The broken pieces fell from her hands, making her think of all the many splintered fragments that made her up, and wiped her hands on her jeans.

"I'm going to stay around, probably work at Green Factory operating machinery like my old man. At least until Isabelle finishes school. Then, who knows?"

She blinked her eyes, but tears began to fall from them anyway. What she wouldn't give to have someone look out for her, someone who cared enough to keep her safe. Wasn't that what a parent was supposed to do? Neither she nor Jack had a parent, not really. She wondered if it was worse to have one and then suddenly not or to never have had one at all? She didn't have any say in any decision he made for himself and his sister, but sadness filtered through her as she thought of all he was sacrificing. Kids aren't supposed to go through what he and his sister—and even she—were dealing with. She wanted to cry for all the children mistreated and abused by those they thought would love them.

"Hey." He moved closer, tipping her chin up. As he looked down at her, a wry grin took over his mouth. "What's wrong with you?" he asked quietly. "Your eyes are leaking."

A shaky laugh left her. She tried to pull away, but his grip tightened. One hand came around her back, pressing her against him. She couldn't suck enough air into her lungs. There was something in his eyes that held her in place, some indescribable emotion that was like a punch to her chest. Whatever she saw there was *deep*, earthshattering, and something she didn't understand.

His head lowered until they were at eye-level. His pulled her even closer, until there was nothing between them but their clothes. Her arms moved, her fingers threaded through his silky hair. He leaned down and pressed a lingering kiss to her forehead. She closed her eyes and inhaled deeply. Her arms slid around his waist, her head resting against his thundering heart. Lola breathed in his scent, feeling safe in his arms. She was at peace. Nothing else mattered, nothing else existed.

The world disappeared.

THE LIGHTS WERE DIMMED, THE volume was turned down low on the television. Through the window Lola could make out his shape in the recliner, the outline of a beer bottle in his hand. Up and down it went, to his lips and back to his lap. She walked inside and slowly closed the door with a racing heart. The room smelled like beer, like he'd dumped bottles of the stuff on the carpet. Maybe he had. Something more for her to clean up.

She avoided looking in his direction, keeping her eyes down and her head turned to the side as she tried to soundlessly make her way past. She had the crazy thought that if she was quiet enough, if she didn't look at him, maybe he wouldn't notice her.

"Where the hell have you been?" he growled.

She froze. Even in the semi-dark she could see his eyes on her—they seemed to glow with menace. "I was...I was at the park." She inched toward the hallway and the implied freedom of her bedroom.

"School called."

She went still with her back to him. Lola waited, and when he said no more, she turned around. The bottle went to his lips, sloshing beer to the floor as he drank. The bottle went back to his lap.

The strained silence continued. Every second that went by was excruciating to Lola.

Her heart beat so fast she thought it might burst. She was dead. She was so dead. The cool, calm façade was the worst, because that's when he was the meanest. She wondered where her mother was, and then wondered why she even had the thought. She wouldn't do anything even if she was home.

"Seems you forgot to mention having detention the other night. And decided to skip out today. Looks like you got another detention coming too. Stupid kid."

She swallowed, her body trembling.

"Where were you today, *really?*"

"I told you—"

He struck fast, faster than she thought possible. One minute he was sitting in the chair drinking a beer, the next he was standing and a glass bottle was flying through the air, toward her. She ducked before it hit the wall, the spray of beer wetting her hair and skin and clothes as glass fell to the floor around her.

"Don't lie to me!"

Tears swam in her eyes. "I—"

A sound of rage erupted from his lips and he charged. She spun around, nothing but survival in her mind, and took off for her bedroom.

"You Goddamn *whore*! That's what you are! Out whoring around when you're supposed to be in school!"

Lola cried out in fear, bumping into the wall in her haste to get away from him. He gained on her, his feet thundering against the carpet. "Mom! Please! Mom, help!" She banged on the closed bedroom door.

Bob was already behind her and she lurched away. "Your mother ain't gonna help you." His stale breath fanned the back of her neck as his hairy arm lassoed her to him.

She screamed, kicking her feet and pounding her fists against his arm. "Let me go! Get off me!" His grip only tightened, almost like he liked her fighting him.

"You want to be a whore. I'll teach you how to be a whore," he whispered in her ear.

Just like that the fight went out of her and she went limp, fear immobilizing her. *Oh, God. Oh, no.* He didn't say that. She heard him wrong. *He didn't say that!*

"Bob? What's going on?" her mother asked from the doorway. She had a grocery bag in her hand, and no expression on her face.

He released her and she fell to the floor on her hands and knees. "Nothing. Just having a chat. Lola had detention the other night and skipped out of school today. Trying to shake some sense into her is all."

She stared at the carpet, not seeing it; shaking and sick to her stomach. *"You want to be a whore. I'll teach you how to be a whore."* She dry-heaved and ran to the bathroom.

What little she'd eaten for lunch came back up. She wet a washcloth with cold water and held it to her face, sitting with her back against the wall. She couldn't stop shaking, her body jerking with the force of it. Never had she been sexually threatened before. Her mind went back to the other night when he'd paused outside her bedroom door. She was scared, more scared than she'd ever been in the past. She could deal with the physical and verbal abuse; she would rather die than have him sexually abuse her. The thought of his foul breath and unclean flesh churned her stomach and she wretched once more. It was like his stench had seeped into her skin to become a part of her.

A knock sounded on the door and she sucked in a sharp breath. "Lola? Are you okay?"

Her lips trembled and she began to cry. *No, I'm not okay. I'm never going to be okay while he's in our life!* She put a hand to her mouth to block out the sound of her sobs.

"Lola?"

She rocked back and forth, tears dampening her face and dropping to her shirt. The sobs became louder, more forceful, and she buried her face in her lap and put her arms over her head. What a waste. What a waste of an existence. This was what she was supposed to have for a life?

"Please, Lola. Are you okay?" Her mother sounded tired—not really worried, not really upset, just tired. Why was she even asking her if she was okay? Why was she pretending to care?

Help me, Mom. Please. Please, help me.

She worked to steady her breathing, dashed a hand over her wet eyes, and said, "I'm...fine." She couldn't keep the tremble from her voice, nor the crack from sounding at the end of her words.

I'm not fine. You know I'm not fine. Show me you care. Show me I still mean something to you. Fight, Mom, fight for us. Fight for me. I'm your daughter! Why won't you fight for me?

It wasn't long before her mom said, "Okay," and the sound of her light footsteps went down the hall.

She stared at the white wall above the toilet for a long time, resolution finally straightening her spine. So that was it then. Her mother was gone. She wouldn't help; she *couldn't* help. And Lola couldn't help her either, not if she didn't want help.

No one could help Lola but herself.

She had to do something. Continuing to live this way was impossible. No more. She wasn't going to take it anymore. Her jaw clenched. She wasn't going to give him the chance to rape her. *Never.* She slowly got to her feet and walked to the mirror above the sink, staring at the haunted girl with fire in her eyes. She told her to be strong, to be brave, to do what she had to do.

She took a quick shower, not able to stand the lingering odor of his sweat and body odor on her flesh, scrubbing her skin until it was pink. She tightly wrapped a towel around her and paused to listen, not hearing any sounds outside the door. She cracked open the bathroom door to silence. Maybe Bob had left. Maybe her mom had gone with him. She didn't even care anymore.

Cold determination propelled her to her room and Lola hastily threw on some clothes, not looking at what she grabbed from her dresser. She didn't think; she just acted. She looked around for something to barricade the door with for her last night in the house. The only thing feasible was her dresser. It took all her strength and anger to get that heavy wood dresser across the room and in front of the door, but she did it.

She grabbed a duffel bag from under her bed and shoved clothes into it. She would go to the bank tomorrow, get her savings, and get out of Morgan Creek. She didn't even know how she would leave, but she was determined to find a way. There were no cabs, no buses in a town this size. *Hitchhike then. Walk. Anything.* She didn't know where she would go or what she would do; she just knew she had to leave.

What about Jack? You're going to leave without telling him goodbye?

Lola shoved him from her mind and the pain that came along with the knowledge she may never see him again. She barely knew him—they hadn't spent enough time with one another to mean anything to each other. Still, she couldn't deny the ache that formed in her chest at the thought of never talking to him again, seeing his smile, hearing his sardonic, yet somehow vulnerable words, or feeling like she was home just by standing beside him.

He'd deal with his life, just as she had to deal with hers. He knew how it was. He wouldn't blame her. No goodbye to her past, no goodbye to her present, only a clear path to the future. That's all she could afford to focus on. Otherwise she would break down and cry, be weak, stay with her mother because of all she used to be and not what she was now, and endure.

No. She refused.

She packed her writing and a framed photograph of her mother and father holding her when she was one year old. Lola put a hand to her mouth as she traced their images with her eyes. *That* was her family. And it didn't exist anymore.

I'm leaving. I'm leaving you, Mother, and I'm not coming back.

CHAPTER 6

LOLA SPENT THE NIGHT WIDE-EYED and jumpy with her ears trained to hear every whisper of movement and her eyes searching the dark for a predator that wasn't there. She periodically dozed off, but continually shook herself awake. It was a long night. She got up when she heard them return from work early in the morning, quietly dressing in a pink top and faded jeans. She looked over her room to make sure she hadn't forgotten anything she needed. She stood there with sorrow as her companion. Was she doing the right thing?

Part of her wanted to try to talk to her mom again, to plead with her once more to leave him. She wanted to tell her what he'd said to her, how she feared he meant to sexually harm her. So many times in the past she'd tried to tell her mother things and she'd brushed them off. She feared today would be no different, no matter what she told her.

You have to do this. You have no other choice.

She waited until she heard the click of their bedroom door closing down the hall, her eyes sweeping one last time over the room she'd considered hers for years. Lola would never stand in this room again; she would never have to lay eyes on Bob Holden again either. Elation and sadness fought inside her. She was saying goodbye to the abuse, but also to her mother.

She grabbed her duffel bag, slowly opened the window, and climbed out. The brisk air stung her flesh. She jumped to the crunchy grass, closed the window, and looked around. The sky was gray and cloudy with streaks of pink in it. She ducked down as she raced past their window and stopped on the sidewalk, her eyes fixed on the dark house. Her breath left her in short bursts of air. She was doing it; she was really doing it.

Her eyes shifted to Sebastian's house, blurring with tears. Her throat tightened as she looked at the window on the second floor, knowing he was there, probably still asleep or just getting up. The longing hit her suddenly and took her breath away. She said a silent goodbye and turned down the street, toward the woods. She would wait there until the bank opened.

HER EYES WENT TO THE slab of stone and she swallowed, disappointed to find it empty. *It's better this way.* She told herself that, but it didn't *feel* better. She hadn't felt a connection with another human being since her lost friendship with Sebastian. Jack had been in her life a very short amount of time, but that time had been significant. He'd eased the pain a little, made her feel not quite so useless and a waste of space. He'd made her smile, made her laugh, made her forget.

She set her bag down and climbed up the rock, the coolness of it seeping into her. She crossed her legs and stared into the dense forest of trees, thinking of the first time she'd known things weren't right. It had been such a small incident. Lola had taken too long in the shower. Bob had been furious because she'd taken an eleven minute shower instead of a ten minute one. He'd banged on the door, shouted at her, and punched the wall while she was in the bathroom. She had been stunned at first—unable to comprehend his reaction to what she had thought was a non-issue. Soon after that, the fear had found a home inside her. It hadn't left since that day.

Lola took a deep breath and slowly exhaled. Her mother had tried to calm him down. Later she'd reprimanded her for being selfish. The next day there had been a timer in the bathroom set to go off at exactly ten minutes. Last night had been a small rebellion on her part not to use it. Not that he'd known.

But she had.

Tears turned the trees into dark blobs. She brought her knees to her chest and wrapped her arms around her legs. From that moment on, her mother had sided with him regardless of how irrational he was. She didn't know if it was to keep him pacified, or because she just didn't care about his treatment of Lola enough to stick up for her, but Lana had acted like all the problems were because of her and not because Bob was messed up.

After a while, her mom just hadn't seemed to care *what* was going on, so lost in herself and her own inability to deal with the situation going on around her that Lana lived in a fog. *Oh, Mom. How could you let this happen to us?* Her shoulders shuddered as a sob left her. So alone. She was so alone. She looked up, eyes stinging, and checked her watch. It was time to go.

By the time she reached the bank, the temperature had raised considerably. With the month of May, heat came into Wisconsin. Lola removed her jacket and shoved it into her duffel bag. She took a rubber band from her wrist and pulled her hair into a loose ponytail. Outside the small gray building, she got her savings account ledger and account number ready and went inside.

It smelled like apples in the bank and the clickety-clack sound of fingernails against keyboards surrounded her. The interior was shades of tan and gold and overabundant in flowery plants. One other customer was in the bank; an older man caked in dirt and grime. He nodded to Lola and she nodded back.

She was greeted with smiles and hellos from the ladies on the other side of the counter as she approached an older lady with white curls, glasses, and a pleasant smile. The nameplate read 'Mary'.

"Hello. How can I help you?" Mary had kind brown eyes that had the power to make her teary-eyed.

She blinked and turned her head away until she had control over her emotions. She took a deep breath and set the ledger on the counter. "My name is Lola Murphy. I'd like to withdraw my savings, please. Here's the account number."

The bank teller took the ledger and went to the computer. As she typed, her pleasant expression turned blank. Mary looked up, brows furrowed. Before she said anything, Lola knew something was wrong. Panic squeezed her chest. "What is it?" she whispered.

"I just need to check something." The teller gave a tight smile. "I'll be right back."

While she watched, Mary went from behind the counter and into an office where a man sat at a desk. Through the window they exchanged words. Both looked at Lola. They talked some more as they looked at a computer screen.

The lady returned. She wouldn't look at her as she said, "Your account has been closed, Lola."

"What? Why? I don't...I don't understand." A buzzing began in her ears and dizziness caused her to sway on her feet. She put a hand on the counter to hold herself up.

"Your mother came in yesterday afternoon and closed it." Mary's eyes finally met hers. "I'm sorry."

Her voice seemed to come from far away and the world went gray. She shook her head and lost her balance. Gone. Her money was gone. Her mother took her money. *Bob* had her mother take her money. She grabbed for the counter and missed, stumbled back a few steps until a chair stopped her. She was trapped. She couldn't leave. She had to go back home. She had to see him again—she had no choice.

Despondency hung her shoulders. Tears blinded her eyes. She backpedaled toward the door, ignoring the looks of concern from the tellers. Once outside, she dropped to her knees, too overwhelmed to care who saw her or what they thought. Lola openly sobbed, her throat and chest tight. What did she do now? She was stuck. And he was only going to get worse.

"Are you okay?" someone asked. She ignored them until they went away.

She got to her feet on legs that shook. It seemed pointless to go to school. What did school matter when she was living a life of abuse at home? It seemed small in comparison when the big picture was so awful.

Maybe I should just end it. End it all. No more pain, no more worry, no more sadness, no more fear.

A sense of relief washed over her. Peace, even. Maybe it was the only solution. It would be so nice not to feel anymore, to just cease to exist. Would anyone really care anyway? She'd be forgotten within months, like she'd never been. Lola walked home, numb. Nothing registered. No sounds, no sights, nothing. But something happened along the way. Something seeped into her, took over, and *consumed* her.

It was rage.

She wasn't ready to give up, not yet.

She entered the house and tossed the duffel bag to the side. She strode for the bedroom her mother and Bob shared. She didn't knock; she just pushed the door open and let it bang against the wall. It was musty and hot in the room and her stomach revolted. Her eyes went to the bed, to their sleeping forms. Her upper lip curled in revulsion. *Hate you, hate you so much.*

Bob snorted and shifted under the covers. Lola walked over and kicked the bed with her shoe. Maybe she was making it worse, but then, how could it get any worse? At least she was finally sticking up for herself. When he didn't move, she kicked the footboard again, backing away as he sat up. His face was red and puffy; his thinning hair surrounded his head in black tufts. "What the—"

Her hands fisted and opened, fisted and opened. "You stole my money."

He sat up, blinking at her. "What did you say?"

Lola's mom mumbled something as she reached for Bob.

"Get up, Mother."

Lana jerked awake into a sitting position. Her eyes were bloodshot and her hair stood up on one side. "What's going on?" she asked, eyes going from her daughter to her husband and back. "Why aren't you in school, Lola?"

"Don't you talk to your mother like that." His eyes narrowed on her. "And we better not be getting in trouble for your truancy. Get your ass back to the school."

Disgust for him twisted her features, disgust for her mother followed. She turned eyes that blazed on him. "You … stole … my … money."

His lips twisted cruelly and she was stunned by the depth of her revulsion for another human being. "I needed it."

"I *earned* that money. It was *mine*. And you just…*took* it." She turned to her mother. "How could you do this? How could you let him do that?"

Lana looked away. Her throat hurt with the force of her betrayal. Part of her had been hoping her mother hadn't known, somehow, but her silence confessed her guilt. Tears seeped from her eyes, dripped down her face and to her shirt. Her mother was just like him. She didn't want to believe it, but she was. And she was *so weak.*

"Taking care of you ain't free, you know, and we've been on hard times. Not that you would know or care. Needed it for expenses." He scratched his hairy chest. "Now get out of here. We need to sleep."

"Bob lost his job last night, Lola. We need the money for bills. We'll put it back when he gets another job. Please understand," she pleaded, a hand outstretched.

She looked at her mother's hand and wanted to spit on it. Her jaw clenched as she looked her over. "You took the money out *yesterday, before* he lost his job. You're pathetic. Both of you."

Her eyes dropped to the blanket, hiding her shameful face.

Bob fell out of the bed in his haste to get out of it. He swore, untangled the sheet from his legs, and headed for her. "You worthless kid. You think you can talk to us like that?"

She trembled, but straightened her back and looked him in the eye. It was like staring at pure evil.

"You've been nothing but trouble since I married your mother," he ranted, getting close enough to her that she could smell his stench. His hands stretched out and grabbed her arms, his fingers digging into her flesh. "You good for nothing little shit. Mouthing off like that. Nothing but trouble. You're nothing but trouble, you hear me?" Her teeth slammed together as she was shaken like a rag doll.

"Bob. Please," Lana called from the bed.

She stared at him, loathing oozing from her very being. *Do your worst.*

"She needs to be taught a lesson," he said, glaring at Lola.

"Like how you're going to teach me how to be a whore?" she shot back, unable to stop the words in time.

His eyes widened. "You little bitch," he said under his breath.

"Bob? What is she talking about?"

His hands left her arms and immediately went to her throat. She pulled at his hands, but they wouldn't budge. He squeezed and she fought to breathe. "You're lucky I don't kill you," he whispered.

She closed her eyes, willing him to do so and end her misery.

"Bob!" Lana said in alarm. She watched over Bob's shoulder as her mom finally got out of the bed and rushed over to them. "Let her go. Please."

She couldn't move—could barely breathe. The pressure disappeared as Bob finally released her. She sucked in a staggering breath of air, her hands flying to her neck. "Get your ass out of here before I change my mind," he said for her ears only.

Lola stared at him, imagining all kinds of horrific ends to his life.

His fist punched the wall above her head and she flinched. "*Now!*" he roared.

"I hate you. I hate you both," she said evenly, though she was quaking on the inside.

Bob backhanded her across the face and Lana cried out. Lola glared at him, placing a hand to her stinging cheek. Each word, each touch—they helped build her mountain of loathing for him. One day, he would get his. She didn't say anything more, but she thought things. Oh, the things she thought.

CHAPTER 7

LOLA WENT TO THE WINDOW and opened it from the outside. She climbed inside, shut the window, and went to the mirror. Her hair was wild, as were her eyes. She didn't recognize the girl staring back at her. She looked crazy, out of control. There was an unnatural light in her eyes, a set to her jaw not normally there. A glance at the clock told her it was second period at school. She maneuvered the dresser back to its spot along the wall, putting all her anger and hurt into it, picturing it was Bob, and shoved with all her might.

"What the hell is all the racket?" he shouted through the door, banging on it.

She fisted her hand, strode to the door, and slammed her hand against it once. There was a moment of silence and then she heard his retreat. Her breaths left her in fast, shallow bursts. He was going to be abusive to her whether she behaved or not, whether she did something right or wrong. Her head lifted and her back straightened. There was no point in being scared. The abuse would happen regardless.

All she had left was the ability to fight back.

The fear melted away. She felt lighter, freer. She put on makeup for the first time in close to a year. The shadow of a bruise was taking the place of the one above her eye, only this time on her cheek. Her neck was unmarred, at least for now. Lola fixed her hair and grabbed her backpack.

She walked down the hallway of the school like a new person. She didn't clutch her books to her chest and avoid eye contact. She looked straight ahead and strode with purpose. The bell sounded, signaling the end of second period. The gym door opened and there was Sebastian with hair damp from a recent shower. He had on a black buttoned-down shirt and dark blue jeans with black boots. He paused when he saw her. Roxanne wasn't far behind him, arm wrapped around one of his, clinging to him. She had on a tight red shirt and jeggings with brown boots up to her knees.

Lola's newfound confidence fledged. She swallowed.

"What the—" Roxanne began, but cut off when he gave her a look.

Kids bustled around them, propelling the trio into the hallway more. She stood there for a moment, not sure what she should do. Then she saw him. Jack ambled down the hallway, hands in his pockets. He wore a black tee shirt with the word 'Muse' on it and jeans. His eyes zeroed in on her, looking at her like she was the only person in the hallway. Her heartbeat picked up. One half of his mouth curved and her palms turned sweaty.

"Hey. I was wondering where you were," he said, eyes searching her face. They lingered on her cheek and thin lines formed around his mouth. Then his gaze lifted to her eyes and asked a silent question. She gave an almost imperceptible nod. She was okay.

"Lola?" Sebastian was watching them like a hawk, taking in their exchange. "Did you need to talk to me about something?"

She remembered Sebastian then. He stood near her, almost hovering over her protectively. He didn't look happy. And behind him was Roxanne, silently fuming and promising retribution.

"Uh...no," she said, her eyes on Jack.

"Let's go before we're late. Some of us don't especially *like* detention." Roxanne tugged on Sebastian's arm.

Jack gave Roxanne a mocking smile. She pursed her lips, but otherwise pretended he wasn't there.

Sebastian seemed to shake himself. "Right." He gave Lola a lingering look. "If you need anything..."

She didn't respond, well aware of how Roxanne would react to her asking him for help of any kind. Not well. Not well at all. The hallway was emptying around them. They left. Or rather, Roxanne dragged Sebastian away with dagger eyes directed at Lola.

Jack's eyebrows lifted. "So...that was fun."

"Hardly."

"You look different today."

"Oh? Must be the new bruise." She started to walk.

"That's not it," he told her. He reached for her hand, halting her. "What happened?"

Lola shook her head. "I can't talk about it now."

"Okay. But when you want to, I'm here."

"And if I don't want to?"

"That's okay too."

For the first time she noticed how long and thick his eyelashes were, saw the flecks of gold in his green eyes. His lips took on a sensual quality that she hadn't realized was there before. She was stunned to find she thought him beautiful.

He tilted his head. "What is it?"

She closed her parted lips as the final bell sounded. "Nothing. I have to get to class."

He slowly let his fingers caress her arm and hand as he pulled away. "See ya, Goody Two Shoes." He smiled and her pulse tripled in tempo.

She hurried to Biology, flushed and giddy and not sure why.

IT WAS THE END OF the school day. Lola had gotten a warning from the principal about leaving school early the other day and showing up late today. She was supposed to bring a note from home excusing her absences. Lola had one in her backpack, already forged and ready to go. Thoughts on what to expect when she arrived home, she wasn't aware of anything amiss until she tripped over something and went sprawling to the hard floor.

Cruel laughter sounded from above her as her chin hit the linoleum, instant fire sweeping through her. Lola's backpack skidded across to the other end of the corridor and was kicked by stampeding feet eager to leave the school. Someone stepped on her hand and a cry of pain left her.

"What the *hell*, Roxanne!" Sebastian shouted, dropping to his knees beside her. He pulled her up, studying her face. "Are you okay?"

"She tripped. I didn't do anything," she said in a rush.

He shot his girlfriend a look over his shoulder. She watched Roxanne go still and took in the details of her face slowly falling. She looked scared and worried.

He tipped her chin up and let out a sigh. "Your chin is split and bleeding. Probably needs stitches." His eyes narrowed. "Did you hit your cheek too?"

She swallowed. His touch was warm, gentle, and familiar. She shook her head. Her chin burned and also felt kind of numb, but it wasn't excruciatingly painful. She put her hand against her chin, surprised to find it wet. She looked at the warm red liquid covering her fingertips and blinked.

"I didn't *do* anything, Sebastian!" she cried again.

His jaw tightened and he turned his head so he could see her. "I *saw* you. She didn't trip. You stuck your leg out and *made* her fall."

"But—"

"Go home, Roxanne." Weariness resonated from Sebastian's voice. "Just go home." He turned back to Lola. "I'll drive you to the clinic. My mom's working today. She'll fit you in."

"I'm okay."

"I don't think you are, and even if you are, I still want my mom to check you out." The hardness in his eyes said he wouldn't be backing down from this.

She allowed him to help her to her feet. He didn't look back at Roxanne, not once. A broken sound came from behind them. Her conscience gave a twinge and she briefly wondered how she could feel bad for someone so abhorrent to her every chance she got. She knew he heard it too in the way his back stiffened. He had that stubborn set to his jaw that was proof he wouldn't be dissuaded from his current thoughts or emotions anytime soon. If Roxanne was smart, she'd leave him be and let him cool down before attempting to talk to him.

"Sebastian," she pleaded, "I didn't mean for her to get hurt."

He dropped his hands from Lola's elbows and whirled around to face his girlfriend. "What did you think was going to happen?"

She had no answer.

"Let's go. I'll get some toilet paper from the bathroom to hold against it until we get there."

They walked down the hall beside each other, just like they had every school day for years. It felt weird. She kept looking at him out of the corner of her eye. He did the same. They didn't speak. He felt like a stranger and she didn't know how just a year had made that possible. But it had. So much had changed. She wouldn't even know where to begin if he asked her what all had.

It was warm, close to seventy out. She squinted her eyes against the sun and looked at him. She felt dumb holding a wad of toilet paper against her chin, especially with kids looking at her oddly as they went down the steps.

"This way," he said, nodding toward the school parking lot.

She followed him, aware of all the greetings he got along the way. He had always been popular. Not so much because he was good-looking and athletic, although that didn't hurt, but because he was a genuinely nice person.

At the car, he turned to her. "I don't know what to say. I can't believe she did that."

I can, was what she thought. But what she said was, "I'm sure she didn't mean for me to fall." *I'm lying. Also, your girlfriend's crazy.*

The interior of the car was clean and smelled like coconuts. 'Between Two Lungs' by Florence and the Machine played from the stereo. Sebastian turned the volume down and looked at her. The longer he continued to watch her without speaking, the more uncomfortable she became.

Lola already felt stupid, but it magnified with his intense gaze on her. "What, Sebastian?"

He sighed and ran a hand through his hair, mussing it. "Nothing." He fiddled with the keys. "Guess I better get you to the doctor."

She caught a glimpse of a tall figure with a face devoid of expression standing near the lilac bush in front of the school as the car pulled out of the parking lot. She glanced back as the car drove down the street, but Jack was gone.

"Do you have to work tonight?"

She jerked her attention to Sebastian. "Um, yeah, I do."

"I'll take you and pick you up when you're done, if you feel up to working."

She thought of her lost money, thought of her plans to get a car, then to escape. It made her sick thinking about it. All that money. Gone. Any check she got she'd have to cash and hide from now on.

"I have to work, and no, I don't need a ride there or back. I'll be fine." Nothing had changed between them because of this one good deed of his.

His grip tightened on the steering wheel. "What did I do?"

She froze, disbelieving of the pain she heard in his voice. "What?"

The car came to a stop outside the blue building known as Morgan Creek Clinic. 'Somebody That I Used To Know' by Gotye came on the radio.

"Fitting, huh?" Bitterness laced his words.

She frowned, confused. "What are you talking about?"

He gritted his teeth and twisted his body so that he faced her. He stared at her, a tick in his right jaw. "What did I do to push you away? Did I say something? Do something? *What?*"

She stared at him. He looked so angry and sad. She'd never been able to bear his sorrow. What hurt him had hurt her at one point. Apparently it still did.

"I honestly don't know what you're talking about." Their gazes met, his doubtful and hers troubled. "I didn't—"

"Is it because of what I said?"

Lola searched her brain, but nothing came to her. "When?"

"The last time we talked."

She couldn't remember the last time they talked. How could he remember that? Why *didn't* she? The air in the car became thick, heavy, and she couldn't breathe. She was suffocating. "I need—"

"God, what is *wrong* with me?" he groaned, thumping his head against the back of the seat. "You need stitches, not to have a heart to heart. Sorry." He jumped from the car, jogged to her side, and helped her out.

The clinic had two doctors and two nurse practitioners; one of the doctors was Dr. Malory Jones, Sebastian's mother. Derek Jones, his father, owned a hardware store in town and that's where Sebastian worked when he wasn't busy with sports and whatever other extracurricular activities he had going on.

The interior was decorated in mauve and forest green. There was a small waiting area, a desk for the receptionist, and three rooms to see patients in. It smelled like lemons in the clinic. Sebastian remained beside her as she registered at the front desk, even though it wasn't necessary. She continually felt his eyes on her.

The receptionist, an older lady with white curly hair and glasses, informed Lola, "Since you're a minor, we need your mother or father to sign a form giving us permission to treat you."

Her stomach plummeted.

"Call your mom," Sebastian urged when she didn't say anything. "Here. Use my phone."

She stared at the black phone, her hand shaking as she took it. When her mother answered, Lola hung her head in relief, speaking quickly and quietly to her. "She'll be here soon," she told the secretary, handing the phone back to Sebastian.

The room she was assigned was painted celery green and had butterflies hanging from the ceiling. She noticed the bruises on her arms when her blood pressure was taken. The nurse eyed them, but didn't say anything. When she left, she got up and went to the mirror, studying her face and neck. Two small bruises where Bob's thumbs had pressed into her throat were visible.

Sebastian came up behind her. Their eyes met in the reflective glass. "Does it hurt?"

For a minute she thought he meant the bruises, but then realized he meant her chin. "No. It feels weird more than anything. Numb."

He took the toilet paper from her, turned her around, and carefully dabbed at the wound with his eyes down. "I miss you." He looked up at the same time her stomach dropped.

Before she could answer, the door opened and his mother walked in. Dr. Jones was tall, slim, and dressed in a black jacket and skirt with gold heels on her feet. She was a feminine version of Sebastian down to the gray eyes and light brown hair with features more striking than pretty.

Her lips formed into a warm smile and she enfolded her in her arms. "I'm so glad to see you, although the circumstances aren't the best." She smelled like lavender. Lola returned the hug. It felt good to be hugged, to feel loved. Dr. Jones pulled away, took in her face, and her features softened. "Oh, honey, does it hurt a lot?"

She shook her head, wiping her wet eyes on her arm.

"What happened?" She sat down at the desk and opened a laptop.

Lola opened her mouth, but Sebastian spoke first. "Roxanne tripped her."

Dr. Jones looked up from the laptop screen. "Roxanne? Your girlfriend?"

Face red, he gave a tight nod.

She sat back. "I see."

"I don't think she meant to," she said, her words hollow. Two pairs of gray eyes zoomed in on her, showing their suspicion. She shifted her feet. "At least, I don't think she meant for my chin to split open and need stitches."

Sebastian snorted.

His mother gave him a look and motioned for her to sit on the examining table. "Let's take a look."

She complied, the paper crinkling under her as she laid down.

Dr. Jones shone a light on her and brought her face close to hers. "Oh, yes, you do." She paused and looked up at her son. "Sebastian, why don't you step out for a minute."

He straightened. "But—"

His mom raised a hand. "You've been a good friend. If Lola wants you with her while I do the stitches, that's fine, but for now, you need to leave." Her voice was stern.

He stared at his mother and then Lola before nodding. He left, shutting the door behind him.

She moved to sit up.

"You stay right where you are."

She immediately laid back down.

Dr. Jones' face blocked out the light as she scrutinized her. "I've known you since you were four. I read stories to you and fed you. I wiped your nose. I even wiped your behind on occasion." Dr. Jones' image wavered before her as pain tightened her throat. "You've been like my daughter for years. You and Sebastian were best friends, although for some reason you're both being dumb this year. What I'm trying to say is, I would think you could come to me if something was wrong." Dr. Jones cleared her throat when it cracked.

She broke down, tears streaming down the sides of her face. Finally, finally, someone was paying attention. She pulled her up and cocooned Lola in her arms. She clutched her to her, pretending for just a moment it was her mom holding her.

"Now you tell me what's going on and you tell me the truth," she said against her hair. "Who did this to you? Who gave you those bruises?" Her voice shook and she squeezed her close. "Are you being abused?"

It was like a dam broke. Horrible, gut-wrenching sounds left her. She couldn't keep them in, she couldn't stop. Her body was wracked with them, the need to release all her pain unbearable. She rocked her as she cried, stroking her hair and murmuring into her ear.

After a time, Dr. Jones jerked to a stop and said, "Oh, shit, we need to get you stitched up."

She laughed and sobbed as the same time. She'd never heard Sebastian's mom swear before.

"Come on." She patted her hand and handed over a tissue. "Let's go perform some minor surgery. You want Sebastian with you? Of course you do. Come on."

CHAPTER 8

"YOUR MOM STOPPED BY, SIGNED papers, and left. Is there a reason for her abrupt behavior?" Dr. Jones told her, her eyes intent on Lola's face.

Pain stabbed her chest and she looked away from her probing gaze. "Must have...had stuff to do."

"Something more important than being with her daughter when she's hurt?"

She was saved from answering when Sebastian walked into the room. He took one look at her face and rushed over. "What happened? Are you okay?" She was sure she looked quite fetching with her puffy eyes and red nose.

"She's fine. Sit down on the other side of the table—on her *other* side, Sebastian," she said with exasperation. Dr. Jones offered a small smile and gave her arm a light squeeze. "This will sting a bit. Hold still. Deep breaths."

A hand enclosed hers and held it tight—Sebastian's.

"Debbie, is everything ready?" she asked the nurse and was told it was. Her chin was swabbed with a cold gauze pad that smelled like alcohol. "Okay, Lola, here we go." She closed her eyes as the needle came nearer, a sharp sting and pressure letting her know the injection was taking place. It took a few minutes for the area to numb up, a few more for the six stitches to be placed.

"How are you doing? Not going to pass out, are you?" Sebastian asked once it was done.

He still held her hand and Lola squeezed it in silent thanks. "I'm fine."

"Good, because if you pass out, I'll pass out." He paused briefly. "You looked terrible when I first came in. You don't look much better now."

She laughed weakly. "Thanks."

His mother came up behind him. "Okay, Sebastian, time to leave again."

He didn't move, keeping his eyes trained on Lola. "I'm not leaving Lola."

"Yes, you are. Lola and I have some things to discuss. She'll be out shortly."

He released her hand. "I'll be waiting in the waiting area. Fitting, right? Waiting in the waiting area?" At her blank look, he sighed. "Sorry. Lame joke. I'll see you soon."

She nodded and sat up, looking around the white room with its many counters, cupboards, and unusual instruments—anywhere but at Sebastian's mom. She couldn't tell her about the abuse and Lola knew that's what she wanted to talk about. She didn't even really know *why* she couldn't tell her. She wanted to tell her, she really did. And yet she couldn't.

She swiveled around in the chair and looked at her. Those eyes knew. Her lips pressed into a line and she clasped her hands together. "You have bruises on your arms, neck, cheek, and a fading one above your eye. How did you get them?"

She looked at her shirt and fingered the thin material. *Why couldn't she tell her?*

Sebastian's mother let out a sigh. "I can't help you if you won't tell me what's going on. So? What's going on?"

"Nothing." Why did she say that? *Take it back, Lola, and tell the truth.* Her lips wouldn't move, no words would form. It was like her brain shut off.

"Nothing?" Disbelief and disappointment rang clearly in that one word.

She jumped down from the table. "I have to go. I have to work."

Dr. Jones stared at her, incomprehension clouding her features. "Why?"

She purposely misinterpreted her question, knowing she wanted to know why she wouldn't tell her. "Because I'm on the schedule." She walked to the door, opened it, and turned back to look at her. "Thank you. For everything."

SEBASTIAN WALKED HER ACROSS THE street to her house. Her eyes kept going to the door as she wondered what Bob was doing at that very moment—if he was waiting for her. If he would come out and yell at her. Sebastian needed to leave.

"Thanks for taking me to the doctor," she told him and inched toward the door.

"It's the least I could do. After all, it was my girlfriend that attacked you." He tried to smile, but failed. "What time do you need to leave by?"

"I don't need a ride. I'm fine. Really." Fear of what Bob would do or say if he found out she'd gotten a ride from him caused her to sound harsher than she meant to.

He blinked and fell back a step. "Right." He looked away. When his eyes met hers, they were gray pools of pain. "Can we start over? I don't know what happened. I don't even care. I've been miserable this past year. At first I was mad, but now…it just sucks. I miss my best friend."

Her chest constricted. She wanted nothing more than to go back to the year before. Everything had been so much simpler then, better, happier. Lola thought of all the obstacles between them. Roxanne, Bob, her life, and shook her head. They couldn't go back. It was impossible. It was sad, but impossible.

"I'm sorry…I…can't." Her voice trailed off, the last word a barely audible whisper.

His spine stiffened and he turned his back to her. "What's going on with you and Jack Forrester?"

She blinked, wondering where that had come from. "Nothing. He's a friend. Why?"

He swung around, holding her in place with his troubled gaze. "He's bad news, and since when do you hang around messed up people?"

Since I became one.

"There's nothing wrong with Jack. I like him."

He made a sound of derision. "Yeah. I guess I don't know you anymore. You've changed." In a bad way, his words implied.

Anger erupted inside her. "Really? Well, so have you. Since when do you date girls who are *psycho*?"

He opened his mouth, closed it, and then gave a low chuckle. "She is pretty nuts, isn't she?" He laughed. "God, what was I thinking when I got involved with her?"

Lola stared at him, stupefied.

He looked at her face and laughed some more, shaking his head. "I don't know what I was thinking. I just missed you so much and was lonely and Roxanne had been after me for—"

"Forever."

"Yeah. Forever. Guess she wore me down."

"That's great, real impressive." She gave him a thumbs up sign. "Be sure to tell your kids about it all someday. You could start with: Kids, your mom used to be a possessive lunatic, but..."

"She's not *all* bad." Her look said she really was. He smiled and gave a helpless shrug. "I'm weak. What can I say?"

You're not weak. You're strong. I wish I was as strong as you.

"Anyway. No ride then?"

"No"

He shoved his hands in his pockets and hopped off the porch. "I think you just like to torture me."

"What does that mean?" she called after him.

"See you tonight, Lola," he said with a mocking bow.

She watched his lean frame cross the street and continued to watch him until he disappeared into his house. She turned around and went motionless. Bob stood in the open doorway, his eyes on Sebastian's house. He had on a brown shirt and red sweatpants. He was unshaven and his skin had an oily sheen to it. Terror clawed its way up her throat and that suffocating sensation came back to her. He didn't say anything, just stood there, waiting.

She tried to move past him, but he blocked her way. "You remember what I told you, don't you?" he said in a low voice.

She was chilled by the threat in his tone, though she had no idea what he was talking about.

"You remember what I told you the last time that boy showed up here?"

With a racing heart, she stood there, barely breathing. A memory tried to make its way to the surface, but she inadvertently shoved it back down. She didn't want to remember, she knew that. She couldn't bear whatever it was.

"No? Should I remind you?" His voice was even, calm. He *enjoyed* her pain. "Not so big and bad now, are ya?"

She wordlessly shook her head.

"What the hell happened to your face?" he suddenly demanded.

Her eyes flew to his to see if he was testing her. He didn't know. Her mother hadn't told him. Why?

"Fell. Had to get stitches," she mumbled, focusing her eyes on her shoes.

"God*damn* it, girl! All you are is one huge expense after another. Maybe you should start giving your checks to me. Help pay some bills. They're all because of you anyway. Go on now." He moved back just enough to allow her to slide past him. "Get to work and make me some money."

You already took it all anyway.

Lola waited for him to move away more, but he didn't, and she knew he had no intention of doing so. She held her breath, angled her body as far away from his as she could, and sidled inside. His gut rubbed against her breasts and her stomach churned as she hurried down the hall to her room.

"Lola?" her mother called from the living room.

She ignored her, slamming her bedroom door and resting her head against it. What had Bob meant? Why couldn't she remember? Her pulse sped at an alarming rate and she felt hot and cold at the same time. Whatever he'd said was awful, she knew. Dread swam in her stomach and threatened to overwhelm her. She put a hand against her mid-section and pressed. *Don't think about it. Go to work. Don't think about it.*

A knock sounded at the door and she recoiled from it. Lola searched her room; she wasn't sure for what, a weapon or something, and grabbed a book from the nightstand.

Lana opened the door. She had on a pair of jeans and a white tee shirt. Her hair was in a lopsided ponytail, like she'd fallen asleep with it in. "Are you okay?" Her mother pointed to her chin.

"Fine."

"Bob didn't mean to be so rough earlier." She trailed a finger up and down the door, her eyes on her hand.

"I need to get ready for work." Her words were stiff, dismissive.

She looked up. "Oh. Okay." She turned to go. "We'll get you paid back. Don't worry."

"I'm not." What was the point? Lola pulled her work clothes from her dresser.

"Lola?"

She paused and looked up. "Yeah?"

Her mother's lips trembled and her eyes watered. "Please don't hate me."

She clenched her teeth together and willed tears not to come—they did anyway. She stood there, silent and still, until her mother left.

ROXANNE WAS GLARING AT HER again. She sighed and turned away, wishing a customer would show up, anything to keep her busy from her hostile looks and snippy comments. She could actually feel her burning hatred boring two holes into her back. What did she have to be mad about? Lola was the one with fresh stitches in her face.

"How's your face?" she taunted from two checkout lanes over.

"How's your love life?" she returned, glancing over her shoulder just as Roxanne's eyes widened. If Lola was stunned she had said such a thing back, she couldn't imagine how surprised Roxanne was.

Dot laughed and clapped her hands. "Watch out, Roxie, Lola ain't taking your crap no more."

"My love life is *fine*," she said in a voice that quaked.

She ignored her and checked out a customer.

"Too bad *yours* isn't," she continued when the customer was gone.

"Really? Considering *your* boyfriend was with me tonight and not *you*."

Dorothy slapped a hand over her mouth, but the snort was still heard.

"You take that back."

She looked at her. Red eyes in a pale face stared back at her. She'd been crying. It wasn't just fury that twisted her features, though there was that, but it was more. She was devastated.

"After you take back tripping me and my stitches. Not going to happen? I didn't think so."

Her hands clenched at her sides. She stared at Lola for a long time, imagining all kinds of mean things, she was sure. Out of nowhere she burst into tears and ran toward the break room. Amazingly, she didn't feel good about stooping to her level.

She sighed and met Dorothy's gaze. "I feel bad."

"Don't you feel bad. I'm proud of you. Finally stood up for yourself." She leaned over to her. "By the way, he broke up with her tonight."

Her stomach churned. Great. Now she felt doubly worse. On the other hand, it was about time for Sebastian to smarten up. Roxanne didn't return to work and a new boy took her spot. He didn't know what he was doing and kept making mistakes, so at least the rest of the night went by fast as Lola and Dorothy continually had to help him.

CHAPTER 9

THE DAY HAD BEEN TOO long and she was relieved when the cool night air touched her skin. The rattle of a loose muffler caught her attention and Lola looked over the parking lot. The lot was empty, but a black Buick sat idling across the street.

No.

"Lola." She whipped around, relieved and upset to see Jack. He stood near the door of the locked store, his stance laid back until their eyes met. He straightened, his eyes intent on her. "What's wrong?"

The car was put in gear and headed for them. *Oh, God.* Panic shot through her. She clutched his arm and felt his muscles constrict under her fingers. "You have to leave, you have to go." *He'll hurt you. He'll hurt anyone he thinks I'll tell.* She inhaled sharply and shook her head. Where had that thought come from? And why did it make such sense?

He grabbed her arms and held them tightly in his hands. "What's going on? *Tell me.*"

She heard the car slowly approach. Why was he there? Bob never picked her up from work. *Never.* She would be all alone with him, all night. He could hurt her. He could force himself on her. No one would be there. It would be just the two of them. Sick with panic and fear, she stared into Jack's eyes. "We have to go. Please. *Please.*"

He looked over her shoulder, returned his gaze to hers, and nodded. He grabbed her hand and took off at a fast jog with Lola struggling to keep up. She'd never been very athletic and it showed in the cramp in her leg and the fire in her lungs. An engine revved and the car sped up. He pulled her behind the building and into the alley. They zigzagged through yards and alleyways, intent on losing the tailing vehicle.

The headlights continued to follow them.

Lola had the insane thought, *I wonder if this is how deer feel when they're hunted down.*

He suddenly jerked her hand hard and she fell against him. He wrapped his arms around her and pulled Lola into the shadows behind a garage. They stayed that way, locked in each other's arms, their breaths coming out in little bursts of frosty air. A car roared down a nearby street, tires squealing as it took a turn. It sounded farther and farther away until it could no longer be heard. She was safe for the moment. But when she got home—Lola refused to think about it.

She looked up, discomfited to find Jack's eyes on her. The look on his face took her breath away. It was furious and intense; protective. "Who was that?"

"My mom's husband."

"What was he doing there? Does he always pick you up from work?"

"*Never.*" Her body convulsed; fear of the unknown maddening to her senses. She couldn't think about what his appearance at her workplace meant.

He stared down at her with closed features. "Do you think he meant to harm you?"

She shrugged, looking at her shoes. Why was this so hard for her to confess? *Because you don't want others to know your shame.*

He suddenly dropped his arms from her and backed away. "I heard you had to get stitches in your lip."

"Chin." She angled her face and pointed at the strip of medical tape on her chin.

"Good thing Sebastian was there to take care of you."

Lola heard the scorn in his tone and didn't understand it. "What do you have against Sebastian?"

Jack lifted his arms out, palms up. "Nothing. Nothing at all. I'm glad you have someone so great to turn to." His voice was at odds with the words leaving his lips. *Someone unlike me*, he seemed to imply.

She blinked eyes that burned, looking at the grass black with night. She didn't have someone to turn to, someone who understood what she was going through. Lola's gaze collided with Jack's. At least, she never used to. She wanted to tell him he made her feel special, she wanted to tell him he made her forget, that he was the *only* one she could turn to. She didn't know how to put into words how grateful she was for him, short though their connection was.

Some foreign emotion started in the pit of her stomach, like a million butterflies flapping their wings, rose up to slam into her chest, and she acted instinctively, fisting his shirt in her hands and yanking him to her. He stared down at her with one eyebrow lifted, daring her, challenging her. Lola tugged him the rest of the way to her until their lips met. Jack's lips were warm and melded to hers perfectly, like their lips had been formed just for each other to enjoy.

The emotions racing through her were tumultuous, frightening, dizzying. He whirled her around, and pressed her up against the garage, his hard body fitted to her softer one. It was hard to breathe, and yet Lola had never felt so alive. That's what she felt with Jack—

alive. She wouldn't let the taint of her step-father ruin this moment—she wouldn't let his cruel words dirty something beautiful.

A low growl sounded from his throat and she shivered in response. His hands went up and down her spine and back to her hair, wiping the touch of Bob from her soul, from her being. The kiss deepened. Her skin flushed and her heart raced. She wanted more than this with him. Lola broke off, afraid of that knowledge.

He stared down at her with dark eyes. His chest heaved and the hands that clasped her arms trembled. "You okay?" he asked in a gravelly voice.

She stood on legs that shook, feeling overwhelmed, but also stronger than she had in a long time. She gave a brief nod. He ran a hand through his hair and let out a deep breath, reaching for her hand as they began to walk. It was no surprise that they headed in the direction of the woods. Houses became spaced more and more apart the farther they ventured. A dog barked, breaking the silence of night. The moon shone large and bright, practically lighting the whole sky up like a big glow stick.

As the quiet deepened, she got more and more uncomfortable. She couldn't believe she'd kissed him. Lola wasn't particularly impulsive. She had only kissed one other boy in her whole life and that had been Sebastian. It didn't count because she'd been eleven at the time and he had been twelve. It had been strictly for experimental purposes. Neither had liked it. But she had liked kissing Jack—a lot. Her stomach fluttered as she remembered the feel of his lips against hers. The wind picked up, blowing her hair around her head. She shivered and wrapped her arms around herself, jumping when an owl hooted nearby.

Jack laughed softly. "Nervous?"

You have no idea. "No. I'm fine."

"You never answered me earlier. Do you think he meant to hurt you?"

Lola nodded, swallowing.

Out of her corner of her eye she saw his jaw clench. He looked away and Lola watched his chest rise and fall. He exhaled deeply. "You don't have to go back."

Her eyes burned. "Yes. I do. I was going to leave. I was going to take all of my savings and I was going to leave this town, Jack. *Today.*" She took a shuddering breath. "He took my money. All of it. Now I'm stuck. I have to go back. I have no choice."

"There's gotta be somewhere you can go, Lola. Someone you can stay with." He paused. "I wish…I wish it was me. I wish I could help you."

She touched his arm. "You do. You have no idea how much just being with you helps me."

"I think I do, actually," he quietly replied.

She looked away from the intensity of his gaze, not sure what to think of the emotion she'd glimpsed in his eyes—not even sure what emotion it *was.*

They didn't speak for a long time as they walked.

Jack finally glanced at her. "I want you to meet someone."

Curious, she asked, "Who?"

"What's your favorite color?"

She opened her mouth, paused, and answered, "Orange. Yours? Let me guess. Black? Who am I meeting?"

"Blue. Like your eyes. The same exact shade, actually. Periwinkle blue. And I'm not telling."

She stopped walking, her chest squeezing. No one had ever paid attention to the color of her eyes so vividly before. He kept his steady pace and she had no choice but to catch up. A smile kept fighting to the surface, and eventually, she let it.

"If you could go anywhere in the world, where would it be?"

She tilted her head. "Australia."

"Really? G'day, mate, and all that?"

"Why not? I like the way Aussies talk. What about you?"

He kicked at a loose rock with his boot. "I'd go to Mississippi."

"Talk about adventurous. What's so great about Mississippi?"

"My mom was born there. I have distant relatives that live there. I'd like to meet them someday."

Something in his voice was off. Lola reached over and grabbed his hand. "Where is your mom?" she asked quietly.

His profile was grim. "Dead." His pace picked up and she knew he wouldn't be sharing anymore with her on that subject. Her heart ached. One more thing they had in common.

"My dad died when I was four."

Jack didn't respond, but she felt the light squeeze of her fingers. She tightened her grip on his hand. They continued in silence. A mile down the road there was an old farmhouse set in a rambling lawn of trees. Even in the dark she could see peeling white paint, shingles rising up, and an overgrown lawn.

Jack walked up two cement steps and looked over his shoulder at her. "I know it's not a palace, but…"

When she didn't move, he motioned for her to follow and went inside, the door banging shut behind him. After a hesitant moment, she followed. The lingering smells of garlic were strong in the kitchen. The room had white walls, old appliances, and a battered table with three mismatched chairs. But it was clean. There was not a speck of dirt in the room, not a cobweb on a wall. The refrigerator hummed and she heard a television from another room in the house.

Lola left the kitchen and found herself in the living room. 'The Golden Girls' was on the TV. The room was long and narrow and shelves that held knickknacks took up one wall. Pictures hung from another. There was a potted plant under a window. A burgundy couch took up a wall; a brown recliner was in one corner, and a tan one in another.

A girl slept on the tan recliner, a purple blanket wrapped around her. She was beautiful with long blonde curls, thick eyelashes, and a bow-shaped mouth. She was a softer, more innocent version of her brother. *Isabelle*. She was the person Jack wanted to protect most in the world. She was the one he forfeited himself for.

There was a closed door to her left. The sound of running water could be heard through the thin door. Lola turned and noted the staircase to the right. That must be where the bedrooms were. The water shut off and her heartbeat irrationally picked up as she waited for the door to open.

Jack stepped out, his jacket gone. He wore a red shirt that read 'Stone Temple Pilots'. It was tight and she could see his well-defined chest through it, his jeans were low on his waist. Lola felt something deep in her belly and looked away.

"She fell asleep waiting up for me. She does every night. I tell her not to, but..." He looked down at his sister, tenderness softening his features. At that moment he was the most handsome boy she'd ever seen. Jack leaned down and gently shook his sister. "Isabelle. Wake up."

She mumbled something and swatted at her brother.

"Isabelle. Come on. There's someone here to meet you."

It was like a switch was flipped. She jerked upright, blinking her sleepy eyes. She looked at Jack and turned her head to face Lola. Her pretty face was wary, suspicious.

"Hi," Lola said, clasping her hands in front of her.

"Hi."

She felt awkward and unsure of what to say. Isabelle didn't seem particularly happy to meet her. She wondered why. What did she know about her, or *think* she knew about her? Lola knew she hadn't been a snob last year, even though Jack had insinuated such. Had she unknowingly snubbed the younger girl at some point?

He nudged his sister and she scowled at him. "Get up."

Isabelle set the blanket aside and slowly got to her feet, glaring defiantly at her brother the whole time. She had a blue pajama top on and matching bottoms. "Happy?"

"Maybe I should go," she said and edged toward the door.

"No." Jack narrowed his eyes at his sister. "Isabelle has been anxious to meet you. She must just be tired and crabby, right, Is?"

Isabelle crossed her arms and pouted. "Well, I *was* excited to meet you. Until you ditched my brother for Sebastian Jones."

She reared back. "Excuse me?"

"What are you talking about?" he demanded.

With great attitude, she informed them, "I saw you guys today. I saw Lola ride off with Sebastian Jones and I saw you, Jack. I saw you after they left."

"Shut up, Isabelle," he warned, his eyes never leaving his sister's face.

Lola stared at Jack as she asked, "Saw what?"

Isabelle shot her a look of animosity and faced her brother. "Don't tell me to shut up. You were sad. You know I hate it when you're sad. She doesn't deserve you, not if she's going to make you sad." Her lower lip trembled.

She didn't know what to think of that. It made her upset to know she'd hurt Jack's feelings, unintentional as it had been, but it also made her happy or something to know he *had* feelings for her that could be hurt.

Jack glanced at her before he directed his gaze on Isabelle. "I wasn't sad. I don't get sad. You imagined it. Drop it."

"Liar!"

His hands fisted at his sides and Jack's face went blank as he stared his sister down, but he remained silent.

"I just want you to be happy. You're never happy," Isabelle cried. She thundered up the stairs and a bedroom door slammed a few seconds later.

The silence after that was thick with discord.

He avoided her eyes as he said, "She exaggerates. I wasn't sad." He shoved his hands in his jeans pockets and faced the television. "I had no reason to be. He was just taking you to the doctor, right? And it's not like we're anything. I mean—"

She rushed to him and pulled him around to face her. Their eyes met for one brief, charge-filled moment. They moved at the same time, lips slamming against lips, arms around one another, hands touching everywhere. She inhaled his scent, her body instinctively reacting. He leaned her back and she lost her balance and fell onto the coffee table. Jack went with her, grunting as his knee hit the wood. She laughed and he kissed her laughter away.

He straddled her against the coffee table, holding her up against him, and looked at her with something like wonder on his face. "I remember the first time I saw you, *really* saw you."

She smiled. "Detention?"

His eyes clouded over and he pushed away from her, moving to sit down on the carpet. "No. Not detention. It was over the summer, Lola, last summer." He frowned at her. He seemed to search her expression for something and was disappointed by what he found. "How can you not remember? How can you not remember me? Was I really that unimpressive?"

Lola felt sick. She sat with her back against the coffee table and looked at the television. There were holes in her brain, in her memory. Had she suppressed things too terrible to think of? And what did that mean about Jack? Was he part of the bad memories? Even as she thought it, she knew it wasn't that. It was Bob. What had he done or said so horrific that she had blocked it from her mind? And what did it have to do with Sebastian and Jack?

"I have to go." She struggled to her feet, hot and clammy at the same time. She needed fresh air.

Jack stood. He didn't say anything and he face was expressionles, but she was quickly learning that when he felt something intensely, that was when he revealed nothing of his emotions. When he appeared not to care at all was when he cared the most.

"What *is* this?" he asked in a low voice. He wouldn't look at her, his body held stiffly away from her.

"What is what?" she asked.

His eyes pierced her then, his eyes that said so much. "Nothing. Never mind."

Lola hesitated, wanting to say so much, but unsure how to begin. She had no idea what she would even say. "Jack, it's not—"

"It's not me, it's you. Yep. Got it." His eyes met hers. "Except I'm pretty sure it *is* me." His lips twisted sardonically. "Too messed up for you, huh?"

She stood there, disbelief freezing her in place. She finally gave a shaky laugh. "You're kidding, right?" Lola went to him and put her hands on his forearms. "That's *not* what I was going to say. You're the *only one* who understands, the *only one*. I was so alone and scared for so long and you made it a little easier to bear. You make me forget. I don't understand what's happening between us. It scares me. In a good way," she added at his look.

He pressed his lips together and nodded, letting his forehead drop to hers, his arms moving to embrace her before falling away. "Me too. My life doesn't suck quite so much since we started hanging out. Sorry. I'm not very poetic."

She drank in the sight of Jack, feelings things she couldn't put names to. She wanted to laugh and cry; she wanted to run to him, and at the same time, run as fast as she could away from him. Her fingers itched to trace the line of his cheekbone, to feel the softness of his lips against her flesh. She wanted him to hold her, and she wanted to fall asleep within his arms. Jack touched her lips with his fingers and caressed her cheek. Lola turned her face into his palm and closed her eyes. A sense of peace flowed over her, sheltered her from her world.

After a moment, he dropped his hand. "I'll walk you home. I have to let Isabelle know. Be right back."

She examined the framed photographs while he talked to his sister. There were four of them; all of Isabelle, and two with Jack as well. No mother, no father. His expression was somber in each of them, his eyes were large and sad. Isabelle had a small smile on her lips and her brown eyes shone. Complete opposites of one another in looks and dispositions. It was plain to see that even as a small boy he'd carried a heavy burden on his shoulders. Lola stared at his younger image with an ache in her chest. If only she could take some of the burden away. She cocked her head. Maybe she did.

HER UNEASE INTENSIFIED THE CLOSER they got to her house. She pictured Bob waiting up for her, drunk and ready to retaliate for her fleeing earlier. Her feet dragged and she became quiet. The streets were empty, lights in most houses out for the night. It was past midnight and the temperature had dropped considerably.

"You don't have to go back."

She glanced at him and saw that he was serious. "Yes. I do. I have nowhere to go."

He stared across the street to Sebastian's house. "I hate this, Lola," he muttered.

Her gaze followed his. Sebastian sat on the porch swing of his house, watching them. His face was in shadows, but she could feel his eyes on her, the hurt and incomprehension rolling from him to her. He stood—waiting for something, waiting for her.

Jack looked at her with a neutral expression on his face. "Is there anything I need to know about you two?"

Her eyes widened and she shook her head. "No! Nothing like that. We just...we used to be best friends, but we don't talk much anymore and...it's awkward. With everything at home, I just..."

"Pushed everyone away?"

"No," she denied. His eyebrows lifted. *Don't kid a kidder*, that look said. "I don't know. Maybe. I can't remember," she finished lamely.

"That seems to happen to you a lot," was his dry response.

Not until Bob Holden it hadn't.

He lowered his head to look her in the eye. "If he hurts you, you call me, okay? You have my phone number."

She nodded, anxiety accelerating her pulse. She didn't want to go inside. Lola never wanted to go inside that house again. Jack understood. He knew what could happen.

He spoke in a low voice, "I don't want to leave you. You promise me you'll call me. *Promise*."

Her head jerked in what would have to pass for affirmation.

He exhaled loudly. "If you can't get to a phone, you go to him." He nodded in Sebastian's direction. "Promise me." Jack's tone was urgent, his fingers dug into the flesh of her arms.

A lump formed in her throat. She whispered, "I promise, Jack."

He stared down at her, wiping cheeks she hadn't been aware were wet and turned his back on her, fading into the shadows of night. Lola watched him go, feeling bereft. It felt like a part of her, the best part, had been severed.

Sebastian reached her and touched her shoulder. "Everything okay?"

She looked at him. He had on pajama pants and a sweatshirt and his face looked tired. She didn't answer. She didn't feel like lying.

"I was waiting for you. I was worried about you."

She searched the house for signs of movement, for the glow of a television screen. All was dark. He was in there, waiting for her. She shivered, knowing it to be true.

"Lola?"

She took a deep breath, glancing at him.

"What's going on? Are you and Jack dating or something?"

"I don't...know," was the best she could come up with.

"How do you not know that?" He turned away, muttering, "We used to tell each other everything. Now you won't even answer a simple question." He gave her a look full of frustration. "Why won't you give me a straight answer ever? If you never want to speak to me again, fine. If you want me to leave you alone, I will. But I have to know why first. Can you at least answer my questions? What *happened?*"

She swallowed and finally allowed her eyes to meet his. Sebastian had the saddest look on his face. How did she tell him she'd had no choice? It was suddenly hard to suck air through her lungs. Lola felt dizzy. It was her fault. She'd been the one to cut their ties. But she'd had to because of Bob. He'd taken *everything* away from her. Why couldn't she *remember?*

His eyes pleaded with her to know the truth. How did she tell him that? Lola couldn't. "You didn't do anything," she choked out.

He exhaled noisily and shoved a hand through his hair, causing it to stick up. "I must have. You don't just stop talking to your best friend of how many years without a reason, without a *damn* good reason."

She wanted to tell him. Lola wanted to tell him everything. She literally *ached* to do so. She saw him as the child she remembered from pictures; chubby with a cowlick on the crown of his head. She saw him as the six year old who stood up for her when someone pulled her hair in kindergarten. Hot tears dripped down her cheeks.

"What is it?" he asked quietly. "Talk to me."

She remembered her first kiss, awkward and sloppy at the age of eleven and shared with Sebastian. She saw him as he was at fourteen, holding her close when her cat Lucy died, even helping her bury her and attending the funeral in her backyard. A sob escaped her and when she swayed from the weight of sorrow, he caught her. He squeezed her, his arms like gridlocks around her. Sebastian was warm and smelled like laundry detergent, like home. His chin rested on her head. He was always trying to save everyone.

Lola didn't hug him back, but she pressed her cheek to his chest. She'd missed her friend so much. She owed him an explanation, she knew. Maybe someday Lola could explain everything. Not now, but someday. It felt so different from when Jack's arms were around her and that gave her pause. His arms felt right wrapped around her, while Sebastian's felt like a betrayal to Jack in a way.

"I have to go. He'll ... I have to go." She pulled away. "Just ... Sebastian ... just know you never did anything wrong. You were always a good friend to me. The best," she vowed.

His eyes searched hers. "Why are you talking past tense?"

Lola backpedaled. "I...I don't know. I didn't mean to." She tripped over the curb and faced her house, Sebastian already forgotten. It was surreal how her instincts were screaming at her that something bad was about to happen.

Heart pounding, she took a step toward the door. Maybe he would be passed out. Maybe he wasn't there. The car sat in the driveway. He was there. A bitter taste formed in her mouth, that of dread. The house looked the same as it always did, yet seemed ominous. A sense of foreboding followed her up the sidewalk and to the door.

It was too quiet. Her pulse quickened and her throat went dry. Something terrible was going to happen. Lola shoved the thought away. *Everything will be fine*, she lied to herself. She fumbled with the doorknob with a hand that shook. It took her three times to get it open. The air inside was stale and it was so dark she couldn't make out anything. Lola quietly closed the door and stood still until her eyes adjusted.

When they did, a scream was torn from her lips.

CHAPTER 10

BOB WAS RIGHT IN FRONT of her, blocking the hallway that led to her bedroom. Lola couldn't see his eyes, couldn't see his face. Blackness, like his soul, had taken over his features. He didn't speak, didn't move, and for one dizzying moment, she wondered if he was even awake. Then he reached for her, the smell of body odor and beer coming with him.

"You thought you were pretty smart earlier, huh, with your boy toy? Running off like that. What did you think was going to happen when you got back?" His sweaty hand encircled her bicep and squeezed so hard she winced.

She couldn't breathe and felt like she might faint. Bob was drunk and furious. He was going to hurt her—bad.

"What you been telling your boyfriends? What'd I tell you would happen if you went blabbing to people?" He shook her.

"I didn't tell them anything!" she cried. She pushed at his hand, crazy with fear, but he only tightened his grip.

"Then why'd you run off like that, huh? *Huh?*" Saliva hit her face, along with his putrid breath, and she gagged and turned her head to the side.

Do something, Lola.

"Let me go!" Survival instincts kicked in and she renewed her efforts to get free. He was strong, stronger than his unfit body let on, and so much stronger than she was.

He turned her and slammed her against the wall. Her head bounced off it, pain exploding behind her eyes. Lola closed her eyes as dizziness crashed over her. Her legs buckled and all that held her up was Bob. "I told you I'd hurt them if you talked. You want me to, don't you? You *want* me to hurt them," he snarled close to her ear.

Lola fought the blackness that wanted to take over. His words came from far away, a distant memory flooding to the surface.

"You tell anyone, anyone at all, and I'll kill them. I'll hunt them down and kill *them. People have accidents all the time. Sebastian could have something go wrong with his car. Rachel could get food poisoning. All kinds of bad things happen to good people every day. It would be such a shame, a tragedy, for ones so young to lose their lives. You don't talk to them. You don't even look at them. They don't come here. You don't go to their houses. Nothing. You talk to no one. They no longer exist to you."*

A broken sob fell from her lips. Bob was pressed against her, his lower half against her stomach. *Oh, God.* A whimper fell from her lips. Lola felt vile, unclean, trapped. She couldn't think straight, couldn't move. *No. No, no, no.* "Please," she begged, tears choking her and falling from her eyes. "Please, don't."

His breathing was heavy, his perspiring face against her neck. "I'll teach you all kinds of things your little boys have no idea about. You'll like it. I know you will."

This isn't happening. This is a nightmare. I'm in my bed, sleeping. This isn't happening. She felt herself shutting off, going numb as his hands groped her and squeezed her tender flesh. Jack's words echoed in her head. She clung to them, clung to the sound of his voice. *"You promise me you'll call me, Lola. Promise. If you can't get to a phone, you go to him."*

She thought of Jack, thought of his strength. She thought of Sebastian, so close and still unattainable. No one was going to help her. *You have to fight. You have to fight. Fight!* Jack's voice shouted inside her head. Lola cried out and bit his neck, her teeth sinking into the salty flesh. She tasted blood and her stomach roiled.

Bob bellowed in surprise and pain, his grip slackening. She brought her knee up and he roared, his hands dropping completely off her to grab himself. "You little bitch! I'll kill you for that. You're dead!" he shouted in a voice higher than usual.

She fled for the front door. He went after her, tripping in his haste. He fell, his hand catching her pant leg. Lola tried to shake him off, kicking at him and connecting with flesh. *Get to the door and get outside. Get to the door and get outside.*

He raged at her, promising pain and suffering. His grip tightened on her leg and he jerked her toward him. She lost her balance, her head hitting the coffee table as she fell, almost immediately blacking out.

LOLA'S EYES FELT GRITTY. THEY fluttered opened and saw nothing but black. She tried to move, to sit up, and couldn't. Panic set in. She didn't know where she was, she didn't know why she couldn't move. She tugged her arms and legs and realized she was spread-eagle with her limbs tied somehow. Her last memories caused her to retch and she turned her head as bile came up her throat.

She was on a bed that smelled like him. Lola inhaled deeply and gagged once more. Panic rose as she realized she was in their bed—in the bed Bob slept in. Lola began to weep. He was going to rape her. He was going to violate her and no one could help her, no one knew, no one was able to stop him. She wanted to die.

The hot tears trickled down her cheeks to dampen the sheet beneath her. *Please, let me die. Just let me die now.* She tried to bring up rage, tried to hate her mother for bringing him into their lives, but it was too much effort. Despair and horror kept her immobile. Her body trembled with fear and cold. She looked down and saw her shirt was ripped down the middle and her jeans were gone. Nausea built within her, choking her.

When she heard his footsteps, her eyes widened, her breaths becoming frantic. Sobs burst from her lips. Lola wasn't able to control them and the keens got louder as he got closer. She struggled against the bindings, launched her torso from the bed. Again and again she fought, but it didn't do any good. She cried out in frustration. Run down, she lay there panting, flinching as she felt his presence beside her.

"That's good. Wear yourself out," he said quietly.

She stared at him, tried to make out his features, tried to look him in the eye. If Lola could make eye contact, maybe he wouldn't be able to go through with it, but she couldn't see his eyes. It was like staring into an abyss of evil blackness.

"Please! Don't do this. Please. I'll do anything you want."

"I know you will." The bed sank down beside her from his weight.

Her throat was closing—no air could get through. She struggled to find words. "Don't do this. I'll be good. I promise I'll be good. I won't talk to anyone ever again," she babbled, her words frenzied and overlapping.

"You won't tell anyone," he said, tone soothing.

She sobbed uncontrollably, cringing when his fleshy hand touched her breast. Lola shook her head from side to side, wrists and ankles burning from her tugging at them. The straps didn't budge. Bob kneaded the sensitive flesh, squeezing until she cried out in pain. "No," she moaned when his hand went lower. She clenched her thigh muscles, trying to close her legs against his disgusting touch.

His breathing turned heavy, sounding excited, and she closed her eyes as she prayed for unconsciousness. "Relax. Enjoy yourself."

When his hand touched the inside of her thigh, something snapped inside her. She opened her mouth and screamed; short, horrible sounds, over and over. She couldn't stop. Bob yelled at her, tried to put a hand over her mouth, but she jerked her head away from him. The cries wouldn't cease, they sounded inhuman, like an animal. She *felt* like an animal—a trapped, abused, wounded animal. On and on they went, never-ending, full of pain and despair.

Suddenly he was gone. Shouts vaguely registered in her brain, but her own screams blocked out everything. Blinding light pierced her eyes and she averted her head, trying to disappear within herself. Someone was pulling at her wrists, another person at her legs. Her face was grabbed and Lola tried to bite the hands.

"Lola. Lola, it's me," an urgent voice told her.

Her eyes searched for Bob, a low whimper leaving her. Where was he? He was hiding, ready to jump on her, ready to hurt her. She tugged away from the hands trying to hold her and stumbled into the corner of the bed, the wall at her back, and knelt there, quivering. She saw faces, heard voices, but nothing registered over the buzzing in her ears.

"What did he *do* to you?"

"Get a blanket. Cover her up."

A groan sounded from somewhere in the room. A grunt followed.

"Sebastian, that's enough."

"It's not *nearly* enough."

A face was before her, hands were reaching for her, and she lashed out, shoving with all the strength she had left. He kept coming, holding something in his hands. It took her a while to realize it was a blanket from the bed.

She vehemently shook her head, slapping at it. "*No!*"

"Lola. It's okay. I'm just going to cover you up."

Her body tensed and she screamed, "*No!*" Not that blanket, not the blanket that smelled like Bob.

The blanket was dropped, but he didn't go away. What she was seeing finally began to register in her mind. Gray eyes, thin lips. Sebastian. *Safe.* Overwhelming relief washed over her. Lola's eyes rolled back in her head and she went limp.

A WORRIED FACE PEERED DOWN at her. Lola flinched and tried to sit up, but hands gently pushed her down. She was on a cot, in an open ambulance. There was a lot of equipment she couldn't name surrounding her and it made her feel claustrophobic.

"You're safe now," Dr. Jones told her, smoothing a hand over her forehead.

She looked around, seeing flashing lights and strangers. "Where is he? What's going on?"

An EMT climbed into the vehicle. He was thin with red hair and brown eyes. His features were dispassionate, as though he saw things like this all the time and had become immune. "My name is Chris. We need to take some vitals, Miss, and then take you to the hospital to get you checked out."

She stared at him, not really seeing him. Sebastian's mom spoke to him and he glanced at Lola before nodding and hopping from the ambulance.

"Where *is he?*" she asked again, her voice sharp with unease.

"He was taken away by the police. He can't hurt you again," was her grim reply.

"How did you...?" She couldn't finish the question. What if they hadn't gotten there when they had? Her body jerked with convulsions and she was cold, so cold.

"We heard your screams. We were still up, talking. Sebastian was worried about you. He wanted to check on you. He said you'd just had a conversation and it had worried him. He said you weren't acting right. I told him…I told him not to bother you. I told him I was sure you were fine." She swallowed, looking out into the small crowd gathered in the yard. "I never should have let you go back to that house, not after seeing what I did today. I called Social Services as soon as you left the clinic. They told me someone would be over soon to talk to you. It wasn't soon enough. This never should have happened. How could your mother let this happen?"

She clutched the brown blanket covering her, feeling sick. She'd had the same thought so many times, but it was strange hearing someone else ask those words. "Where is my mother?" Her voice was weak and full of strain.

"She was called. She'll be at the hospital, I'm sure." She put her face close to hers and looked her in the eye. "You'll have to talk to the police. You tell them everything, understand? Don't be scared. He can't hurt you anymore. You tell them the truth." She didn't look away until Lola gave a faint nod. She pulled her into her arms and held her tight, placing a kiss on her head. She smelled good, clean. "They're ready to take you now."

Panic soared through her and she clutched at Sebastian's mom, not wanting her to leave her. "I don't want to be alone. *Please.*"

The EMT waited outside with his eyes trained on the ground to give them a semblance of privacy.

Dr. Jones gave her a smile, her eyes wet with unshed tears. "You're not alone, honey. You've never been alone. We'll be at the hospital waiting for you. I promise."

She nodded, but her thoughts were already moving on to Jack. She wanted him with her. Her lower lip trembled and tears formed in her eyes. Dr. Jones got out of the ambulance and the EMT went about hooking Lola up to things. From where she reclined she saw two figures standing outside the ambulance. One was taller, rangier; the other more muscular and not quite as tall—Jack and Sebastian.

Sebastian climbed in and stared down at her, emotions flickering over his face like lightning. He swallowed and grabbed her hand, his grip almost painful. She knew there were things he had to ask, needed to say, but what came out of his mouth was, "I called Jack. I knew you'd want him here."

She nodded wordlessly, tears choking her.

His mouth opened and closed as he looked at her. Lola watched him, wondering what he was thinking. "I'll see you soon." He dropped her hand and left.

Jack entered the ambulance and crouched beside her. He didn't speak, just looked at her with the fiercest expression on his face. He reached over and clasped her hand within his, bringing it to his lips.

"Make it quick. We need to go," the EMT said.

He nodded, his eyes trained on Lola.

She blinked back the tears that threatened to consume her. "I heard your voice," she whispered. "I heard your voice and it gave me strength."

He averted his face for a moment. When he looked at her again, his eyes were red. "I hear you voice all the time," he told her.

She let her eyes close, exhaustion finally taking over.

LOLA HAD BEEN EXAMINED, TESTED, photographed, and talked to by the police. It had been nerve-wracking and painful to put to words the horrible events. Talking about it made it real. Her tongue had stumbled over words, feeling thick and numb—like her. She felt numb.

She was alone for the moment, in a white hospital room that smelled like bleach. A dim light cast shadows about the room, making her uneasy. Lola had to stay overnight for observation since she'd hit her head and passed out. It seemed she may have a slight concussion. There were bruises on her as well. She was stiff and sore and a little dizzy, but none of that compared to the pain inside her.

Rest was what had been recommended by the hospital doctor. Though it was well into the middle of the night, Lola couldn't. Every time she closed her eyes she saw Bob, felt her skin crawl like he was in the room with her, touching her once more. She felt impure, tainted. A scalding hot shower hadn't helped. All the soap in the world couldn't seem to remove the smell of him from her flesh, his touch lingering even now.

She didn't want to think about what would have happened if Sebastian and his mother hadn't found her. Lola shuddered and took a deep breath. *But they did. Remember that.*

The door opened, admitting a nurse. Her name was Molly. She had blonde hair and a cheerful smile on her face. She wore pink scrubs for her uniform and smelled like bubblegum. "Getting some rest?"

She looked at the blanket twisted between her hands. "No. I can't sleep."

Empathy shone on her face as Molly patted her shoulder. "I understand. I'm going to take your vitals again, okay?"

"Is my mom here yet?"

Molly finished up, the blood pressure cuff making a ripping noise as it left her arm, and shook her head. "Not yet."

Her stomach dropped and she couldn't meet the nurse's eyes. Her mother had been called hours ago. Why wasn't she there? Lola's throat tightened.

"I'm sure she's on her way." The nurse paused, and then asked, "Do you need anything?"

She shook her head and the nurse left.

Dr. Jones soon took her place; her expression and tone no-nonsense. "You need to rest."

"I *can't*. Every time I close my eyes I see him. I can still feel him...*smell* him." She shuddered, a bad taste in her mouth.

"Okay. It's okay." She sat down beside her and rubbed her back. Lola rested her cheek on her shoulder. "I'm sorry I failed you."

She pulled away. "What?"

Her face was guilt-stricken. "I let you down. You didn't feel like you could come to me. For that, I'm sorry."

"I couldn't go to anyone. He threatened me. He...he..." Her strangled voice cut off. She couldn't breathe.

"Shh. Easy. Easy." Dr. Jones made a circular motion between her shoulders, soothing her. "Don't think about it."

"Where's my mom? Why isn't she here?" She heard the pain in her voice, the broken quality of it.

"I don't know. She'll be here soon. And...I know it's not the same, but...*I'm* here. And I'll help you any way I can."

She wiped her face and turned to her side so that her back was to Dr. Jones. She just wanted to be alone. She was so tired and so *heartbroken* over everything.

She sighed. "Sebastian and I have to get home. But I'll be back in the morning. Sebastian doesn't want to leave, but I'm making him." She gave a little laugh. "Stubborn boy." When she didn't respond, she sighed once more and got up, the door clicking shut behind her.

Hot, hated tears streamed from her eyes onto the bedding. Lola stared at the wall across the room, trying to figure out what could possibly be the reason her mother remained absent. She must blame her. That's why she wasn't there. Nothing else made sense. She was going to believe Bob's side of the story. Lana was picking him; a cruel, malicious, *evil* man, over her own flesh and blood.

Lola bit her fist to keep a sob inside, her shoulders shaking from the effort it took to restrain it. Her mother didn't want her. She didn't love her. She couldn't. How could her own mother sacrifice her and for what—for *him*? It shouldn't hurt anymore; she should be used to it.

It still hurt and it always would.

CHAPTER 11

STARTLED BY THE GENTLE TOUCH on her shoulder, she jerked to a sitting position.

Jack was there. There were brackets around his mouth and eyes, like he was in physical pain. He didn't say anything. He never had to say anything. Lola already knew. He moved closer, pressed his forehead to hers and inhaled slowly, deeply. She closed her eyes, savored the smell and touch of him—his presence.

"They wouldn't tell me anything. Did he...?"

She immediately knew what he meant. She averted her eyes and shook her head. He would have, though, given the chance. That knowledge filled her with repugnance, fear, and dread.

"I want...to kill him," he bit out through barely moving lips. His jaw was set, his nostrils flared with every shallow breath he took.

"Jack—"

He swung his head around to pierce she with eyes that flashed black. "I shouldn't have let you go back. I wish..." He turned his back to her, shoulders tense. "I wish I could take you away. I wish I could take you away from all of this."

Lola flinched at the shattered look on his face, lowering her eyes to her lap.

"You never deserved this. You know that, right? Lola? *Lola.*" Strong hands gripped her shoulders. "This isn't your fault. You didn't do anything wrong. Look at me. Look at me." She finally did. "You didn't do anything wrong."

"I know...I know that, in my head. I know this isn't my fault. But it feels like it is too. Maybe I said something, maybe I did something. I mean, why would my *mom*...want someone like *that* over *me*? And what did I do to make him act like that toward me?" Her lips trembled and her eyes burned with unshed tears. "What's wrong with me?"

He sat down on the bed and pulled her half on his lap and into his arms. She inhaled his faint cologne, feeling safe. His body was ripcord hard and lean against her; strong and sturdy like Jack.

"And my mom." Her voice broke. "Why didn't she stop him? Why didn't she take my side over his? Why didn't she *protect* me?" Her body convulsed and his arms tightened around her. "She's not here. She didn't even come." She wept, wetting his shirt with her sorrow. "How could my own mother not come see me after what happened? Am I unlovable? Am I a horrible person? Is that what's wrong with me?"

He pressed his jaw to her forehead. "There's nothing wrong with you. You don't *ever* think that way, Lola. It's him. It's all him. And your mother. She's *wrong*—wrong for letting this happen, wrong for not being here. No parent should forsake their child. No parent should let this happen to their child. Don't ever think you did anything to deserve what happened to you. And you can't make your mom what you need and want. She should be ashamed, not you. Never you."

"What about you?" Lola wiped her eyes with her fingers.

He went still. "What about me?"

She moved back far enough to see his face. It was grim as he waited. "Do you realize that about you and your sister too?" His face closed. "It's not your fault."

"We're not talking about me," was his clipped answer.

She put her hands on his face and forced him to look into her eyes. "It's not your fault either. You're a good person."

His lips went into a thin line and he looked down. "That's me. Good Samaritan through and through."

"You *are*. You've helped me so much. I mean, yeah, you act all cocky and tough, but there's sweetness to you. I've seen it, with me, and with your sister. And I...I wanted to die at times. I thought it would be better. It would be easier." He gave her a sharp look. Lola felt ashamed to admit such a thing, but she had to say it. Jack had to know.

She grabbed his hands and held them between them. "I felt like I died the moment the abuse started. I lost myself. I lost *everyone*. And then you called me Goody Two Shoes and brought some fire back into me, some life back into me. I didn't start living again until you showed up. It was like...I was...*reborn*. In your eyes, in the way you looked at me, the things you said to me, the things you didn't even have to say. Thank you for that. Thank you for giving me something when I felt like I had nothing."

"But I didn't do anything good!" He tugged his hands away and stood, pacing the length of the bed. He repeatedly ran a hand through his shaggy hair, tousling it. "How can you *not* remember me? I wasn't *nice* to you. I was cruel. I was *wrong*."

She fell back against the pillow. "I don't understand." Her heartbeat picked up. She didn't want to know, didn't want to hear anything that might change her feelings for him. He was the one constant, the one person she knew she could count on above all others. "What are you talking about?"

Don't tell me. Tell me it doesn't matter. Tell me to forget about it. Don't tell me.

He stared at her, frustrated. He shook his head, looking away. "Last summer. You came to the rock." He sighed and faced her. "You really don't remember?"

"No. I wouldn't say I didn't remember if I did. What happened?" *Why was I there, of all places? No wonder the place seemed familiar. And why did I block it out of my mind?*

He hesitated. "It's not a good time. Not now. Maybe I should go. You've been through a lot and you need to rest."

Lola fought down panic. "I don't want to be alone. Not now, not yet," she said in an unsteady voice. She wanted him to stay, but she couldn't be selfish. Jack had obligations at home, someone who needed and depended on him more than she did. "Your sister? Will she be okay?"

"Yeah. She knows I'm here. Isabelle is fine. My dad will go straight to bed when he gets home from work. He always does."

"So...stay. Please?"

He grimaced. "You may not want me to after I tell you."

"It can't be that bad." *Can it?* She straightened her spine and gave him a level look. "I've had a horrible day. It can't get much worse. Just tell me and get it over with."

Jack laughed gruffly and ran a hand over his face. "I was at the rock. You showed up." He was hedging and she motioned for him to get on with it. "You were crying." His voice softened and took on a bleak quality. He expelled a noisy breath. "My dad, he...my dad knocked me around good that day. Needless to say, I wasn't in the finest mood."

She waited with bated breath, captivated by the inflections in his voice and the altering expressions on his finely chiseled face.

"You didn't see me at first." Jack had a faraway look on his face. "I watched you for a while. You were so sad, so beautiful and tragic."

He thought she was beautiful?

He closed his eyes. "I didn't like how you made me feel. I know it was immature. I was feeling sorry for myself, you showed up crying. I felt...I don't know what I felt." He sat down in the lone recliner in the room, partly in shadows. "I felt *something* when I saw you looking like that, something I had never felt before, something that scared me."

She listened intently to each word, not wanting to miss something or hear anything wrong.

"Then I told myself you were probably upset because you broke a nail or some equally trivial reason. You didn't know what real pain and suffering was or what it felt like to be knocked around." He made a sound of self-deprecation. "God, I was an idiot."

"You didn't know."

He looked up. "You're right. I *didn't* know. I didn't know a single thing about you, other than what was common knowledge at school. I should have known better than to jump to conclusions. I of all people know how that all works."

She was as guilty of that as he was. Lola felt ashamed of her assumptions of Jack and his character before she'd gotten to know him. She'd been so wrong, so very wrong. A memory tickled her mind and faded away. "You said something to me, something that was unkind."

"You could say that."

"It doesn't matter." Lola meant it. She one hundred percent knew it didn't. But to Jack it did. He obviously needed to expunge his shame. She kept quiet, waiting for him to continue.

"I implied you were easy, something about your newest boy standing you up, and not to cry because I was sure you had lots more guys lined up. It wasn't good. Even as I said the words, I wanted to stop them, but they just kept coming." He got to his feet and moved to the end of the bed. He stared at her, regret radiating from him. "The look on your face...it hurt me so much it was like I was hurting myself, or my sister. It was horrible. I'd never felt so little, so small. I felt like my dad. I hated it. I don't *ever* want to be him. To get off on other's pain. To hurt people. I'm so sorry, Lola."

She picked at the blanket, her eyes on her hands. "The reason that day is so terrible for me, the reason I blocked it out, wasn't because of you. I barely remember that exchange. I was too upset by what happened before that."

He didn't say anything, so Lola continued, "Bob threatened my friends that day. He told me if I told anyone about the abuse, he'd kill them. He said he'd kill Sebastian. And Rachel. And anyone else I talked to." Fear reared up inside her and she wondered if it would ever completely go away. Was she ever really going to be safe?

He pulled her into his arms before she'd realized he'd moved and kissed her on the lips, his mouth moving to her jaw, her cheek, her neck—little flutters of tender warmth against her skin.

"I..." Jack began, stopped.

"What?" she whispered against the ebony silk of his hair.

He crushed her to him and she felt the pounding of his heart against her own. "You're safe, I promise. I'll keep you safe. No matter what."

"I know." And she did.

"Do you still want me to stay?"

"Yes."

Another nurse came in to take her vitals. Jack sat in the chair, waiting. As soon as she left, he got into the bed and pulled her to him, tucking her head under his chin. She fell asleep like that, more peaceful than she had been in months.

SHE NEVER CAME.

That was her first thought when she opened her eyes.

The second was, *Jack's gone.*

She sat in the hospital bed, blinking sleep from her eyes. Streaks of sunlight came in through the window and formed shapes on the bedspread covering her legs. An overbearing amount of sorrow repeatedly lapped over her like waves of heartache, unending and paralyzing. She vaguely remembered waking up throughout the night, terrified and shaking, sure Bob was coming after her. Each time Jack murmured comforting words and held her close. But he was gone and the alarm began to trickle back into her veins. What if he had been let out of jail? What if he was waiting to hurt her more? Or worse, someone she cared about? She shoved the troubling thoughts away, telling herself it would be okay, she would be okay.

The doctor came in to check her over. Everything looked good and he told her the release papers would be signed later that morning. *Where will I go?* Her mother had abandoned her. That hurt more than anything Bob had done to her. Tears, ever present lately, flowed from her eyes. Lola was still wiping her eyes when the door opened. Two women walked inside, the first one short and plump with straight brown hair. She had a brisk look to her that was slightly alarming.

"Hello, Lola, I'm Veronica Smalls and I work for Social Services." The alarm grew, turned to panic.

The other woman caught and held Lola's attention. She hesitantly walked over to the bed, her eyes trained on Lola. She looked nervous and sad. She frowned. She also looked familiar.

"This is Blair Murphy." *Murphy?* Her heartbeat picked up.

The lady was petite, slender, and had wavy auburn hair much like Lola's, but kept shorter. She was pretty in a quiet way and dressed in jeans and a green top. She smelled faintly of cinnamon. "Hello, Lola," she said softly, coming to a stop near the window. The sunlight played with her hair, highlighting red and gold tones.

"Lola, your aunt Blair is going to take care of you for a while," Veronica informed her, stepping up to the bed.

The woman continued to talk, but none of it registered with her. She stared at the woman she had just been told was her aunt—her father's sister. Lola unconsciously touched her nose and chin, seeing the same features on the woman standing before her. She winced as the tender flesh newly stitched reacted negatively to her touch.

"Wait a minute," she interrupted. "Where's my mom?"

Veronica pursed her lips. "Your mother is signing over guardianship to your aunt, at least temporarily. She can't take care of you right now."

The room faded and flared back in blinding white. Her ears buzzed. "What? I don't understand."

The brusque woman turned to Blair. "I'll let you two get acquainted. Someone from Social Services will be in touch."

Her aunt nodded, waited until the older woman left, and then turned to Lola. "This must be...odd for you. I know a lot has happened to you. I thought, um, maybe we could talk for a bit?" She tilted her head, studying her.

Lola didn't say anything.

She cleared her throat and seemed to shake herself. "I guess I'll go first. I live here in Morgan Creek. I have for the past eleven years."

Two years after Lola moved there. She'd been so close this whole time.

"I write a column for a women's magazine. I've never been married. I have two cats. I like funny movies and Chinese food. Let's see..." Blair seemed to search her brain. "My favorite color is green."

"What are their names?"

She blinked. "What?"

"Your cats. What are their names?"

"Oh." Blair smiled a true smile and a dimple appeared in her left cheek. "Piper and Larry. Both males."

"Why did you name them Piper and Larry?"

"Well, Larry is after an ex-boyfriend. He had a shoe fetish. Particularly *my* shoes, I should add. I caught him trying on a pair once. He was a little...strange. We broke up shortly after that." She giggled and Lola felt a small smile stretch her lips. It fell from her lips almost immediately. It didn't seem right to smile after the events of the past night.

"Larry, the cat, that is, likes to sleep with my shoes. He wraps his paws around them like a teddy bear and sleeps that way." She shrugged. "It just fit. I honestly don't know how I came up with the name Piper. I think I heard it on a movie or something."

She looked at the blank television screen as the quiet dragged on. She had so many questions that she didn't know where to begin.

Blair stood and pulled her shirt down. "I imagine you're wondering why you haven't met me before now, living in the same town and all."

"Yes. Why didn't you contact me sooner? You've been here this whole time…" Her voice trailed off. She frowned as resentment and confusion battled inside her.

Her aunt crossed the floor and stopped beside her. There were such varying glimpses of pain on Blair's face that Lola felt a tightening in her chest. "I'll explain everything, in time. But first, I want to make sure it's okay with you that you'll be staying with me. I realize we don't know each other, but I would love to be given the chance to change that." Blair lifted a hand, made a fist, and let it drop to her side. "You look so much like your father," she whispered, her brown eyes shimmering with tears.

"What about my mother? Why doesn't she want me?"

Her eyes shifted away. "It's not that she doesn't want you, Lola, she's just incapable of giving you proper care right now."

It felt like someone had punched a hole in her chest, ripped out her heart, and left her like that, wounded, bleeding, and beyond repair. She'd had it all figured out in her imaginary world where wishes and hopes and dreams come true. Her mother would show up at the hospital. She would tell her she was sorry and they would never see Bob again, never have to deal with him again. In spite of *everything* her mother had allowed, she was still her mother. She still needed her, messed up or not. Lana had carried her in her womb for months, brought her into the world, raised her, and most of the time, had been a good mother to her. What had happened to the mother she remembered from her childhood? Why had she changed? Or had Lola recreated a childhood in her mind that hadn't existed? No, that couldn't be true.

She forced herself to meet her aunt's gaze. "When can we leave?"

She watched her for a moment. "I'm so sorry," Blair said in a voice low with regret. "I'm *so* sorry all of this has happened to you."

Lola shrugged, though the hole in her chest was widening with each passing minute. "Yeah. I keep hearing that from people."

After a pause, her aunt said, "I spoke with the doctor. Anytime now the papers should be signed. I brought some things for you. They're in my car. I'll be right back."

Alone, she let out a shuddering breath and forced herself to get up. She stood on legs that wobbled, trying to get her bearings. She couldn't even cry, which was actually a relief. She was so *sick* of tears. Lola's chest hurt as she sucked in another lungful of air. She looked around the sparse, sanitized room, not really seeing it. She went into the small bathroom and showered and brushed her teeth. When that was done, she sat on the bed in a hospital gown and robe and waited for her aunt.

Images of the night before stabbed her mind in horrifying flashes. Lola saw Bob's twisted face, felt his perspiring skin. A heavy weight pressed down on her and she inhaled and exhaled, trying to slow her pulse down. She felt like she was going to be sick.

Blair returned, holding a familiar-looking duffel bad. "Your mother packed some things for you. Whatever else you need I'll buy for you."

"What...about me? Doesn't she want to see me?"

"I'm sorry."

The chasm in her chest widened. She silently took the bag and went into the bathroom. She changed into red pajama pants and a pink long-sleeved shirt, pausing to stare at herself in the mirror.

Her cheeks were hollowed out, and there were dark smudges under her eyes; bruises turning yellow on her cheek and jaw and throat. She raised her face and eyed the black stitches on her chin, which just completed the freak show that was presently her face.

Her mother didn't want to see her.

She turned away from the mirror and left the bathroom. Her aunt put an arm around her as they left the hospital room, offering wordless support. It was a kind gesture.

CHAPTER 12

BLAIR'S CAR WAS A WHITE Chevrolet Cavalier that was spotless and smelled like mint. The ride was quiet, low music playing from the radio. Her aunt apparently liked country music, humming along to the song.

Her house was on the other side of town from Lola's. It was a two-story red house with white trim. It made Lola think of candy canes and Christmas. There was a porch where two white wicker chairs resided and purple and pink flowers bloomed around the house. A large tree stood in the yard, tall and proud. She instantly fell in love with the surroundings. Everything seemed well-kept and homey. It was a house Lola would have liked to live in. She paused at that. She *would* be living there now—for how long, she didn't know.

It felt like betrayal to her mother to look forward to calling such a place home; to be glad to be away from hers, but that house was covered in bad memories and pain. Lola felt such *relief* knowing she didn't have to go back there. Again she felt bad and bitterness slammed away the guilt. None of this would be happening if not for Bob, none of this would be happening if her mother had been stronger, if *Lola* had meant more to her mother than some ridiculous excuse for a man.

"Lola? Coming?"

She shook her head and followed her aunt up the porch steps and through the door. The entryway was open and spacious and smelled like vanilla. To the left was the kitchen and to the right was the living room. The walls were creamy white and filled with framed photographs of scenery and people, some animals sporadically added into the mix. Lola walked over to one, touched in some inexplicable way by the black and white photo of a curly-haired girl with a serious expression on her face, her striking blue eyes the only color in the picture.

"Like it?"

She jumped at the sound of Blair's voice so close to her. She nodded, backing away.

"I'm a freelance photographer in my spare time."

She glanced at her aunt, impressed. She tried to remember hobbies of her mother's, talents she once used faded away over time like her smile. Disturbingly, she couldn't think of any. *Don't compare them*, she scolded herself.

"Come on. I'll show you your room and introduce you to Piper and Larry." She touched her arm and gestured toward the living room. The room was large and again had creamy white walls. There was a bay window that looked out onto the street. It was lovely. Lola could see herself sitting in the bay window with her writing on her lap.

The furniture was navy blue, the curtains blue and tan striped. A Bose entertainment system and a large flat screen television took up a good portion of the wall. Awed by the beauty captured in each photo Lola's eyes grazed, her respect for her aunt grew and she found she wanted to know more about her.

A staircase along the back wall of the room led to the second floor. At the top of the stairs was a long hallway with open doors going down it. The first room was a bathroom, the second was Blair's office. At the end of the hall were two bedrooms.

"Here it is. Your room." Blair walked in and turned toward her with an expectant expression on her face.

She stepped inside, a lump forming in her throat. "It's beautiful," she whispered. And it was.

The walls were mauve and cream striped, the king-sized bed canopied with a lilac quilt over it. The floors were hardwood, and there was an abundance of windows allowing sunlight in. Two dressers stood side by side along one of the walls; a desk and chair resided between a set of windows. Lola thought of the room she and her mother had painstakingly decorated and longing swept over her. She blinked her eyes and averted her face from her aunt's probing gaze.

"Are you okay?"

"I'm fine."

Blair fidgeted. "Well. Um...I'll let you get settled in. Unless you're hungry? Thirsty?"

"No."

She looked like she wanted to say more, but with a resigned nod, her aunt left.

She stared at her meager belongings consisting of one duffel bag and whatever was inside it. She unzipped the bag and removed the clothes and toiletries. She froze, her eyes finding something she hadn't been expecting to see. At the bottom of the bag was a thick purple folder. Her eyes began to tear up and an ache closed her throat. It was her writing. Her mother had somehow known about it and made sure she had it. She hadn't thought her mother had known about her poetry writing.

She sat on the bed, teardrops wetting the folder in her lap.

LOLA AWOKE TO TWO LUMPS of furry warmth by her—one near her head, and the other by her feet. For a disoriented moment she was back to the night before and it was Bob on top of her with fear choking her. Then she remembered where she was. She must have fallen asleep at some point. She sat up and stared down at a large black cat. He blinked up at her with lime green eyes. She looked toward her feet and an equally large orange tiger cat meowed at her.

"Piper and Larry, I presume," she mumbled, yawning.

The black one jumped down, grunting as his stomach hit the floor on the descent. The orange tiger meowed again and rubbed his head against Lola's feet. She stroked his silky fur. "You're a cuddle bug, aren't you? I bet you're Larry."

A knock on the door announced Blair's presence. She smiled and leaned against the door with her arms crossed. "That would be Larry, yes. Piper's a little more standoffish. He likes you."

She shrugged, her eyes downcast.

"I made some lunch. I wasn't sure what you liked so I made tuna salad and peanut butter and jelly sandwiches."

Lola couldn't remember the last time someone had prepared a meal for her and discomfort pierced her chest. "Thank you."

"No problem. Come on." She held out a hand. "You have yet to see the kitchen."

She got up and looked at the hand offered. Small acts of kindness had a tremendous impact on her as she'd received them so fleetingly within the last year. She gripped her aunt's hand and it enclosed around hers, anchoring Lola to her as they walked down the hall.

The kitchen had black and white checkered walls, which of course she stared at. The appliances were red and the floors hardwood. The countertops were black and white swirled marble. There was a table by a row of wall-length windows, and an island with four barstools. It was the most awesome kitchen Lola had ever seen.

"Do you like it?"

She turned in a slow circle. "Yeah," she breathed. "I like it."

Blair laughed a tinkling sound of joy. "Good. I spend a lot of time in here. I love cooking and baking. I'm not very good at it, but I have fun with it. Have a seat." Her aunt motioned to the table. She sat down and her aunt brought over a platter full of sandwiches cut in halves. "Help yourself. What would you like to drink? Water, tea, milk?"

She reached for a peanut butter and jelly half sandwich. "Water is fine. Thank you." She took a bite, savoring the sweet gooeyness of it. It had been ages since she'd enjoyed a PB and J—or any kind of food for that matter. After a few small bites, her stomach revolted, and she set the sandwich down.

"What's wrong?"

"Nothing. My stomach just gets upset a lot."

Blair swallowed and put her tuna salad sandwich down. "Do you want to talk about it?"

Her eyes pricked as she saw the caring in her aunt's. "What was my father like?"

A smile softened her features. "He was a wonderful man, Lola, the best. I wish you could have known him longer."

"I don't remember him at all. I wish I did. My mom says he was a good man."

"He was." Their gazes locked.

She pushed her glass of water back and forth between her hands. "I have a hard time taking my mother's word for it, given her current husband."

Blair got up and took the seat closest to her. She reached over and gripped her hand. "I'm so sorry you had to go through such horrible things. I..." She stopped, shaking her head.

"You what?"

Her smile wobbled. "I just wish I could have been there for you. I wanted to be."

She pulled her hand away. "Then why weren't you? You've been in town almost as long as us. I've seen you around town throughout the years. You've even checked out in my lane at at work. You never once said anything to me, never gave me any idea you were my aunt. Why?"

She didn't speak for a long time. When she did, her voice was low, stricken. "When your father died, something happened to your mother. She just kind of...lost touch with reality. You were so sad, so confused about everything. You didn't understand any of it, your father no longer being around, your mother's indifference. I saw what it was doing to you. You needed your mother and she...it was so hard on her. It was too much.

"I offered to take you, to have you stay with me, just until your mother got better." She took a shaky breath. "Lana lashed out at me, went hysterical. She thought I wanted to steal you away from her. She'd just lost your dad and I suppose the thought of not having you around was too unbearable for her, even if she couldn't give you proper care. It didn't matter to her. She wanted you with her, even if it was in your best interest not to be.

"She forbade me to see you, to talk to you, to have any kind of contact with you. She said if I didn't stay away, the two of you would disappear and I'd never see you again, not ever. It greatly pained me, but I wanted what was best for you, I wanted to believe your mother was doing what she thought was in your best interest, for whatever reason. So I agreed."

Tears streamed down her face, but Blair was seemingly unaware of them. "I moved here to at least be close to you, even if I couldn't interact with you. I've tried talking to your mother throughout the years, tried to get her to see reason. She never relented, not once. It was so hard. Seeing you and not being able to tell you who I was, how much I wanted to know you. So many times I had to bite my tongue not to blurt out I was your aunt. You have no idea the restraint it took." Blair took a shuddering breath.

"I don't know what made her keep me away. Fear of losing you maybe. Maybe it was too hard to see me, a reminder of Joe. She loved him so much. Lana was a different person then." She smiled sadly, swiped at her eyes with her hand. "It seemed like she got better. Never the same, but a semblance of herself. She was a good mother to you, wasn't she?" She took a deep breath. "Or am I wrong?"

She opened her mouth to speak and found she couldn't. She cleared her throat and tried again. "I think she was. I remember her being a good mom, even though she always seemed a little sad. Some days she slept a lot, but not every day. But then...she met Bob and everything changed. I didn't know her anymore. I don't know what happened, what changed. Why she let me be treated that way." She blinked her eyes against tears.

"If I had known what was happening, nothing could have kept me away." She lowered her head until she was at eye-level with Lola. "*Nothing*, Lola."

Her lower lip quivered as she tried to keep the tears inside, but they eventually won. She covered her face with her hands and wept, crying harder still when Blair's hands came to rest on her shoulders, her cheek atop the crown of Lola's head.

"I have some people that have been bugging me to see you. Are you up for a visit or would you rather it wait?" She rubbed her shoulder and gave it a squeeze, pulling away to see her face.

She wiped her eyes. "Who?"

"Well, there was this boy that stopped by when you were napping. He was very insistent I tell you to call him as soon as you woke up."

Her stomach fluttered. "Jack?" she whispered.

"Tall, dark-haired, beautiful green eyes? He's cute." She smiled.

Lola felt her skin heat up.

"Is he your boyfriend?"

"I...don't know." She frowned. What were they? More than friends, definitely. But boyfriend and girlfriend? They'd never discussed it.

"And this morning when I stopped at your house to pick up your things, *another* young man, equally cute, I might add, flagged me down and bombarded me with questions. His mother came outside to tell him to stop pestering me, and then she started." Blair chuckled. "Nice people. The mom is Dr. Jones, isn't she?" Lola nodded. "She wants to come over sometime soon to see you. Her son said he was coming over either way, with or without his mom." She paused. "You have a lot of people that care about you. I wish you would have reached out to one of them."

"Jack knew," she blurted, and then wished she hadn't.

Her aunt's eyes narrowed. "I see."

She jumped to her feet, feeling like she needed to defend him. "It's not like that. Jack understands what I went through and he knew I didn't want anyone to know." She couldn't tell her that he went through the same thing, or even worse. It wasn't Lola's to tell.

"Why didn't you want anyone to know?"

Her chest tightened. "Bob told me if I told anyone, he'd hurt my friends."

"Oh, how awful," she gasped and covered her mouth with her hands.

"And with Jack...I didn't have to say anything. He just knew. He was there for me when I had no one." She took a shaky breath and turned away. She couldn't explain how much he meant to her already.

"I told Jack to stop back in a couple hours. Do you want to help me with something in the meantime?"

Not wanting to hurt her aunt's feeling, she agreed and soon found herself on a mat in the living room, focusing on her breathing and stretching her limbs to their limits. Funnily enough, it helped to relax her and take her mind off her current situation.

She was grateful to Blair, even though she said she hated doing Yoga alone and that was why she asked Lola to participate. She knew the real reason—finally someone was looking out for her.

CHAPTER 13

LOLA SAT ON A BENCH under a leafy tree in the fenced-in backyard. The sun was warm where it touched her skin through the tree limbs. Blair had asked her all her favorite foods and gone to the grocery store to stock up. She hadn't had the heart to tell her she picked at food more than she ate it. Maybe, in time, that would change.

She watched a robin hop along the grass and a butterfly flittered by her face. She envied them both. They were free. Lola was now too, at least physically. Her emotions were so far away from free she wondered if she'd ever find peace. Thoughts of her mom plagued her. Why had it been so easy to give up her rights, to stay away? Probably for the same reason it had been okay for Lola to be abused as her mom sat by, not stopping it, not even seemingly aware of it. That reason would forever be a mystery to her, and something she would never understand.

She resented her so much and missed her just as much. She longed to see her and at the same time never wanted to set eyes on her again. Her emotions were tumultuous where her mom was concerned and didn't make much sense, not even to Lola. Most of all, she just wanted to know *why*. She wrapped her arms around herself, wishing she could fast forward to years from now, when all of this would be behind her and in the past, instead of living through it now.

Her aunt told her Social Services would be coming to talk to her and that she would be assigned a social worker to periodically meet with her. Blair would have to be approved a fit guardian before it became legal. She hadn't said it, but Lola knew she'd probably have to testify against Bob at court. A chill went down her spine. She never wanted to see him again. Would her mother be sitting on his side of the courtroom when that time came? Would her mother have to testify? Would charges be brought against her as well? At least he was stuck in jail throughout the process. That knowledge made her feel a little more secure. She took a shuddering breath and looked up.

She blinked her eyes against the sunlight, breathless with what she saw. She slowly stood, her pulse tripping. It was Jack, standing near the fence gate. His hands were shoved in the pockets of his jeans. He had on a Batman shirt and holey jeans. His hair hung partially over his eyes, his lips curled in their derisive way. She took a staggering step toward him and he quickly closed the gap. Lola devoured his features with her eyes.

He was the most beautiful sight Lola had ever seen.

"Miss me?" he said in that mocking way of his, but the unsteadiness of his voice belied his calm exterior.

Lola inhaled his wonderful scent, a tremulous smile on her lips as they embraced. She clutched him to her, loving the feel of his warm body against hers. It was scary how every part of her being reacted to his presence, to the very sight of him. Eyes closed, she let everything fall away but that very moment. She didn't think, she just felt. Jack's hands went up her back, down her back. His cheek pressed against her hair. His lips grazed her temple. Rightness cocooned them. She loved his touch, his scent, his voice, the way he made her feel.

She jerked away, her eyes trained on him.

His brows lowered. "What is it? Did I hurt you? Is it your chin? What, Lola?"

"I...um..." was all she could get out.

His fingers gripped her shoulders. "Talk to me. Are you okay?"

She wordlessly nodded.

"Then?"

"Nothing. I...I'm just so happy to see you." It was the truth. It was so much more than that, but that was all she was able to put into words.

Jack expelled a noisy breath. He looked away, nodding. "You have *no idea* how happy I am to see you."

Her stomach fluttered and what she was sure was a goofy smile covered her lips.

"I wasn't sure the greeting I would get after what I told you last night."

"Jack, you have no idea how unimportant what you told me last night is compared to everything else going on."

"I don't know if I should be offended or relieved."

She smiled and rested her head on his shoulder. "You didn't say goodbye when you left."

"Sorry about that. You were finally sleeping. I didn't want to wake you. And the nurses kicked me out." He grabbed her hands and held them. "How's your aunt treating you?"

She looked at the house, *her* house. "Good. I like her."

"She seems decent."

"She is." Their eyes met.

"I'm glad." He averted his face as he said, "I have something for you."

She gave him a curious look. "You do? What?"

He laughed and ran a hand through his hair. "It's a surprise. Come on."

"This isn't going to be like last time you wanted me to do something and I met your sister that hates me, is it?"

"She doesn't hate you. She just doesn't know you. Isabelle doesn't trust easily, which you can understand."

"I do."

She grabbed the hand he offered, following him around the house. He stopped beside an old beat up red Ford truck parked along the curb.

"Is this yours?"

He opened the driver's side door and reached inside, the faint sickly sweet smell of farm wafting out. "Technically, it's the farmer's I work for, but he lets me drive it whenever I need to."

"Does this farmer know? About your dad?"

"He suspects." He paused. "I keep to myself, Lola. I do my work and keep my mouth shut. That's the way I want it to be." There was an unspoken warning in his tone to not press. Lola didn't. Jack pulled his arm out, a 10 X 13 canvas in his hands. He held it facing him. "This is for you."

She took it from him with hands that shook, swallowing hard. Jack looked at the ground as she turned it around. She stared at it, overwhelmed by what greeted her. It was her face in black and white. It was her from before—before Bob, before all of this. Lola's eyes shone, her lips curved in a secret smile. He'd captured a part of her she'd lost. It was beautiful, perfect. She was better in the coal drawing, better in Jack's eyes than she'd ever be in real life. The way he saw her was awe-inspiring and humbling.

"I don't look like this," she whispered, tears burning a trail down her cheeks.

"This is how I see you," he answered quietly.

She turned away from Jack, her throat tight with emotion. He gently tugged the canvas out of her hands and pulled her toward him, his lips warm and firm against hers. Jack's body was tightly wound, his kiss passionate and consuming. Her body responded and she kissed him back with all the feeling she had.

LOLA WENT BACK TO SCHOOL after missing a week. People stared. She didn't know if it was because of the stitches on her chin, the fading bruises on her face, or because they knew what had happened to her. Maybe it was all of those things. She felt stupid, like a loser. Things like that were only supposed to happen to kids that asked for it, that were troublemakers and came from poor white trash families. Lola used to be that naïve at one point too and so very *wrong*, but no longer.

One of the first people to approach her was Rachel. She didn't stare at her, she didn't even speak. She grabbed her and pulled her into a tight embrace. She hugged her back, not realizing until then how very much she'd missed her friend. It overwhelmed her and made it hard for her to speak.

"Do you have to work tonight? If not, we're hanging out. No excuses," she stated when she pulled away.

"I don't have to work. With everything going on, they said I could have a few weeks off." Lola glanced around the emptying hallway. It seemed like everyone was watching them, but that couldn't be. "How did you...find out?"

Rachel picked at the hem of her black wraparound shirt, not looking at her. "Everyone knows. Not really sure how it got around, but it did. You know how people are."

She also knew how judgmental, stereotypical, and *mistaken* people could be too. What they thought happened and what *really* happened were most likely two very different things.

The bell rang just as Lola looked up and caught Roxanne's eye. She quickly looked away and strode in the opposite direction.

There had been no animosity in her gaze, which was a first. No Sebastian by her side either.

"Come on, we're going to be late." She tugged at her hand and propelled Lola toward their first class of the day.

SHE LOOKED FOR JACK THROUGHOUT the day, missing him and longing to see him, but not once did she catch a glimpse of him. She was scared for him. He usually only missed school when his dad was especially violent. Lola imagined all sorts of terrible things and by the end of the day, she was in a panic.

She'd searched the halls for Isabelle, but not surprisingly hadn't seen her, which wasn't unusual. Sebastian was another story. He was like her shadow most of the day, an overprotective, over*bearing* shadow. The final bell sounded, signaling the end of the school day and there he was, hovering behind her as she hurried out of the school. The sun instantly heated her, hot and cloying with humidity.

"Lola, we need to talk."

"Not now, Sebastian." She took in the surrounding buildings and trees, wondering if Jack was somewhere near, watching and waiting. She looked for an old truck that had seen better days. Her shoulders slumped when she found not a trace of him.

"Yes, now." He pulled her around to face him. He looked like he was searching for words, like he thought if he said the wrong thing she would break.

"Call me later, Lola," Rachel said with a wave, smiling at her. She nudged Sebastian's shoulder as she passed and Lola didn't miss the way his eyes followed her as she walked away. Interesting.

"I need to..." He sighed, running a hand through his hair. "Can I give you a ride home?"

She searched for Jack once more before giving up and focusing her attention on Sebastian. "Okay." She waited until they were in the car to say, "You know, I'm not going to fall apart."

He nervously fiddled with buttons and knobs in the car, turning the air conditioning on. Almost immediate relief washed over Lola's flushed skin. He pulled the car out of the parking lot, his eyes trained straight ahead. "I don't know what you mean."

"You. *Hovering*. I'm fine. I don't need a bodyguard."

"I want to be there for you."

"Why?"

He glanced at her, frowning. "Because we're friends. That's what friends do."

She took a deep breath and stared out the passenger window. "We haven't talked in a year."

"I know. I don't know what I did to push you away, but I'm sorry."

"*I'm* sorry," she interrupted, twisting her body to face him. "It's my fault. I pushed you away. I thought I was protecting you. I'm sorry for that. But it doesn't change the fact that we haven't talked in a long time. We don't even know each other anymore. You've changed. *I've* changed."

I've changed so much.

The car came to a stop as they reached Blair's.

"I know that. But what *hasn't* changed is how I feel about you. I love you. You know that. You're my oldest friend. Yeah, things are awkward now, but it'll get better." He reached over and touched her cheek. "You've been through something terrible, something you never should have gone through. I want to help you, to be there for you."

She put her hand on his. "You were there for me when it mattered most. Don't ever forget that."

He tugged his hand away and looked out the window. "It never should have gotten to that point. I should have done more. I should have figured it out sooner. The way you were acting..."

"Don't put any blame on yourself. You did what you could and I will forever be grateful for that. For you."

He turned back to her, offering a semblance of a smile. "We'll get through this, and be stronger friends because of it. You just watch."

His optimism was admirable and maybe naïve. She wished she could be so unfailingly confident about it. In her friend's smile, Lola allowed herself to feel hope for the first time in a long time. True, she and Sebastian could never have the kind of friendship they used to have, but maybe it could be *better*—different, but better. The closeness they'd shared was gone and she didn't know if it would ever come back, but there was no reason they couldn't be friends.

Stop pushing people away.

She smiled, a small laugh falling from her lips. Lola reached across the console and hugged her friend, feeling a little more whole. "I've missed you."

He squeezed her to him. "Me too."

"One condition."

He pulled back, grinning. "What's that?"

"Stop being my bigger, more muscular shadow."

"Deal."

She opened the door and got out. Sebastian followed. She immediately longed for the cool interior of the car, her skin rapidly damp with perspiration. They walked up the porch steps. At the door, Lola took a deep breath and turned. There was something she had to say, something they needed to discuss if they were ever going to move on.

"I remember what you said to me the last time we talked, before we completely stopped talking. That had nothing to do with my avoidance of you. You know that, right?"

He averted his eyes. "Yeah. Sure."

He didn't believe her. Was that why Sebastian had kept his distance for so long? Had he been embarrassed? The things he must have thought.

Lola touched his shoulder. "Sebastian, it had nothing to do with you asking me out, although the timing was really terrible."

He looked at her, caught her smile, and shook his head in self-derision. "I tend to have bad timing a lot."

She didn't want to cross-examine that comment. "Is that why you started dating Roxanne? Because you were hurt?"

"Partly." He looked toward the street. "I mean, we were together all the time, since we were kids. And then, *bam*, out of nowhere, you didn't talk to me anymore. Only it wasn't out of nowhere 'cause I'd just confessed to you that my feelings for you were changing and I thought we owed it to ourselves to test out dating."

Lola looked at her tennis shoes. "Only I said I didn't think it was a good idea."

He sighed. "Yeah. There was that." A sad smile formed on his lips. "Like I said, at first I was mad, hurt, and acted like I didn't care that you were avoiding me. I kept my distance too, nursing my wounds."

"Dating Roxanne," she interrupted dryly.

He ignored that. "But, after a while, I really missed my friend. And that's what I realized you would always be. My friend. From the way you were acting, I thought it was too late for us, that we couldn't go back, that you hated me."

"I'm so sorry."

"It doesn't matter now. I wish I had known. I wish you had told me what was going on. I could have helped. My mom and dad too. You're like their kid to them too, always have been."

"He said he would hurt you. I couldn't risk it."

Sebastian stared at her, finally nodding. "I understand why you did what you did. I don't like it, but I understand. I would have done the same, if it meant protecting you."

They were silent, both digesting their exchanged words.

"Can I ask one thing?"

She glanced at him. "Sure. Anything."

"Why wasn't it a good idea? I'm curious."

How did she answer that? She trailed a hand along the back of a wicker chair, choosing her words carefully. Maybe at one point, for one fleeting instant of craziness, she had thought of the possibility of Sebastian being more than a friend, but Jack had completely wiped out any such notions with one surly look and mocking comment. And she was more prone to think it had been loneliness and longing for her friend more than anything that induced the insane thought anyway. It wouldn't have worked. They were like siblings—nothing romantic would have lasted between them.

"We grew up together. You were like my brother, Sebastian. I've seen you pee yourself. You've had my puke on you." Lola smiled when he shuddered. "I guess, we were *too* close, if that makes sense. It's hard to be romantic with someone who knows all the disgusting things you've done throughout your childhood. Does that make sense?"

"Yeah." He laughed. "It does."

She was beginning to feel more like herself again, just standing there talking with him. It was a good feeling.

"So. Rachel, huh?"

He shoved his hands in his pockets, conspicuously not looking at her.

"She's a good person. We've always been friends. She's sweet," she added approvingly.

"As opposed to?" One eyebrow lifted.

"Not going there."

"Probably best." He looked at her. "So. Jack, huh?"

Her face burned. "Yes," she said with a straight back and her eyes steady on him.

He raised his hands and backed away. "Hey. Whatever. I don't know him. I'll have to trust your judgment."

Warmth trickled through her veins and she grabbed Sebastian, spontaneously kissing his cheek. "Thank you."

The door opened. "Hi, guys." Blair smiled at Sebastian and turned to Lola. There was a smudge of flour on her cheek and white handprints on her yellow top. "How was your day?"

It was a simple question. There was nothing significant about it, nothing to cause such a response in Lola. Her eyes watered and her throat tightened.

"That bad?" She sighed and reached for her, rubbing her back.

"No. It…was…fine," she said, trying to steady her voice.

"Then why are you crying?"

She gave a shaky laugh. "I don't know. Because no one's asked me about my day in a very long time."

"Well, expect it now. Lola, there is someone here to talk to you." She gave her a look and her heartbeat picked up. "It's a social worker."

Her stomach plummeted. *Not her mother. Not Jack.* "Oh. Okay."

Sebastian touched her arm. "I'll see you tomorrow. You'll be fine," he added as he took in her features.

She didn't feel like she was going to be fine. Lola felt like she was going to throw up. Or pass out. Or maybe both. She took a deep breath, held the hand Blair offered, and followed her inside.

BY THE END OF THE visit, she was exhausted. She'd had to retell the events that had landed Bob in jail. Each word had been like a stab of pain to her chest. The social worker had been nice and apparently Lola would be seeing Alice Johnson, the social worker, for weekly visits for some time.

An attorney had been appointed to her case as well. She wasn't exactly sure what his role was—he'd said something about looking out for her best interests. She was confused because she'd thought that was what the social worker was doing too.

Then there was the Child Protective Service worker who was performing the background checks on Blair to make sure she was fit to be her guardian and that Lola was safe in her care.

It had been a huge relief to learn she wouldn't have to testify in court. She never wanted to see Bob Holden's ugly face again. But her mother...it hurt so bad she couldn't breathe when she thought of her.

She blinked her eyes as tears formed and tried to focus on her homework.

"You okay?"

She looked up at Rachel's concerned face. "Of course. I just ... this question is hard."

"So hard it brings tears to your eyes?" She leaned across the bed and peered at the Home Economics book. "There aren't any questions, Lola. It's a picture."

She snapped the book shut and tossed it to the side. She wanted to talk to someone, but didn't feel comfortable unloading all of her doubts and fears on Rachel. It didn't feel right. It was weird trying to pick up exactly where she and Rachel had left off. Lola wasn't that girl anymore. It was like trying to wear a shirt that no longer fit. Had she completely outgrown her old life and friends?

"Do you want to talk? Maybe you would feel better."

She did want to talk, but not to her, and she felt bad about it. She shook her head.

"Okay. I can't force you to talk if you don't want to. But you would feel better if you did." Rachel waited, but when she didn't answer, she said, "Since you don't feel like talking, I'm going to because I *do* feel like talking."

Lola looked up, curious.

Her friend tapped a pencil against a textbook. "So...there's this guy I like. And I think he likes me. But I'm not sure how someone else fits into the whole thing." She glanced at her. "Should I be concerned that you're smiling?"

"Of *course* not! This is a smile of happiness."

"Oh. 'Cause it looks kind of demonic."

"Probably because I'm so out of practice." They both laughed, her insides warming with gratitude that they could talk and laugh like they once had. Maybe it wasn't so hard to pick up where they'd left off. Maybe all Lola had to do was open up and let her friends back in.

"Who is it?" Rachel's blush gave it away and her smile widened. "It's Sebastian, isn't it? I would *love* it if you two dated."

"Really? Thanks. That makes me feel better. I was worried."

"Why would you be worried? You're my friend and he's my friend. That would be awesome if you dated. But, there *is* Roxanne to be worried about. I doubt she'd be happy about you two getting together."

She grimaced. "I can just imagine how she'll take the news. Probably send me hate mail or something."

"If you're lucky that's all she'll do." She pointed to her healing chin.

"I still can't believe she did that."

"Indirectly."

She rolled her eyes. "Yeah. She'll probably *indirectly* run me over with her car or something." Rachel glanced at the clock on the nightstand. "I should get going. I promised my little sister I'd watch a movie with her tonight. I'll see you tomorrow." She hopped down from the tall bed and gave Lola a smile.

She smiled back, impulsively drawing her friend into a hug. "Thank you."

Rachel hugged her, pulling back to ask, "For what?"

"For making me laugh, for talking about happy things instead of letting me wallow in sad ones."

"Don't you know by now? That's what friends are for."

"Like the song."

"Totally like the song." She paused. "Just so you know, I think you and Jack are great for each other—for what my opinion's worth."

She blinked, the warmth in her chest expanding. "Thank you," she said softly.

With a wink, Rachel said, "See you later."

Once she was gone, Lola sat cross-legged on the bed with er eyes on the newly hung drawing across the room. Looking at it made her happy and put a smile on her face. Recent life was so different from how it had been not too long ago. Sometimes she thought it couldn't last—others she hoped beyond hope that it would. There was still fear and unease stamped into her, but there were also small measures of what she viewed as a perfect existence trickling into her days in the form of laughter, joy, love, and wonder.

LOLA COULDN'T BELIEVE HER AUNT let her take the car. Throughout the course of every day she was stupefied any number of times by the way Blair treated her—or didn't treat her. The smallest acts of kindness felt like pampering to her and were enough to bring tears to her eyes. And every time her aunt didn't yell at her or hit her for something Bob would have, she felt a little lighter, a little more human.

There was still anxiety fighting inside her and she wondered if that would ever entirely go away. She slept with the light on in her room and the door open. Lola had nightmares most nights and she didn't like to be alone in the house. Her aunt accommodated her as best as she could, working from home when she was able. She was an amazing person and Lola was sad she hadn't been able to know her growing up, but she was thankful she was getting to know her now.

It was dusk out, a grayish pink cast to the trees and grass marking it as such. The rock she stared at was larger than life; the person lounging on top of it even more so. Her pulse tripped just looking at him. Jack was on his back with his head propped up on his arms. Lola got out of the car, looking at his profile as she walked toward him, taking in the straightness of his nose and the way his hair hung in his face. A green shirt, jeans, and boots made up his outfit. The air was humid, hot, and mixed with Lola's emotions, made it hard to breathe.

"Hi," she greeted quietly, putting a hand on the cool jagged stone. Jack didn't look at her. "Hi."

That wasn't exactly the acknowledgement she'd expected. "Where were you today? I didn't see you at school."

"What do you care?" He sat up, his face blank as he turned toward her.

Lola couldn't believe the way he was acting, like she was *bothering* him. "I was worried. I—"

"Don't be."

Sharp pain went through her as she took a step back, stumbling over a broken tree branch. "What's going on? What happened? Is it your father?"

He jumped to his feet, his body stiff as he looked at her. Hi expression was closed—his eyes were dark green with coldness. "I said not to worry about me. Now run along to your new life, with your old friends. I want to be alone."

She hated that tears pricked her eyes, making a ragged path down her cheeks. "Jack. Please. Why are you being this way? What did I do wrong?" she beseeched in a barely audible voice. She wrapped her arms around herself, trying to push the hurt away.

"You didn't do anything wrong," he said in a raspy voice, turning from her. His shoulders lifted with the breath he took. "Look. I get it. You're okay now. You have your aunt and your friends. Sebastian. You don't need me anymore. I helped you through a bad time and now everything is the way it should be. You don't have to feel obligated to continue to talk to me."

"I don't...understand."

He whirled around with flashing eyes, speaking low and slowly. "You're better now. You don't owe me anything. You don't need to feel like you need to seek me out. There's no reason for you to think you need to talk to me because you feel bad for me or something."

She reached for him, but he brushed her off.

"I *saw* you." A muscle ticked in his jaw as he glared down at her. "I saw you and Sebastian. I went to your aunt's house after school and I saw the two of you on the porch."

Lola frowned, uncomprehending. Then she remembered the hug and kiss. How could she explain to Jack that it hadn't been anything he should worry about?

"And maybe it wouldn't bother me so much, if I knew. But I don't. I don't know what's going on with us. I don't know what I am to you. And it's *killing* me." His voice was stark with pain. She never wanted to hurt him—never wanted to cause him pain. He'd had more than his share of it already.

"It didn't mean anything," she said in a voice that wavered. "We're just friends."

"Yeah. And what are we? *Nothing*, right?"

She flinched at his words—at the ache they caused inside her.

Jack swore at the look on her face. "I'm sorry. I didn't mean that. I just—you don't need me anymore and...I guess it hurts. I know it's selfish. You're better and you don't need me, so I should be glad, but I—I still need you." He took a shuddering breath. "I'm no good at this stuff." His shoulders slumped and he turned away. "I'm no good," was the whisper that reached Lola's ears.

She briefly closed her eyes, those words causing an unimaginable hurt within her. She took a deep breath and touched his arm. "You're better than good, and it doesn't matter how things are in my life—I'll need you whether they're good or bad," she said with conviction, never meaning anything more.

He moved for her, pulling her to him. Their bodies collided, their hands all over each other—his lips on hers, her lips on his. Fire sparked between them, consumed, took over. Lola couldn't think. She didn't want to think. It was amazing the way he made her feel. She hadn't realized another human being could make her respond the way she did to Jack. Her body was aflame, her pulse chaotic as her heart pounded against her ribcage.

Please don't end. Don't let this feeling end.

His scent mixed with sweat and became even more intoxicating. Pressing her back against the rock, the front of his body meshed with hers. A low moan sounded in his throat as she pressed herself even closer against him, wanting to be as near to him as she could get, wanting to be part of him. It was scary and thrilling—it was beautiful.

The kissing and touching continued until Jack finally pulled away. "We have to stop," he said with ragged breathing.

She blinked at him through a haze of fog. "What?"

"We have to stop, while we still can," he said slowly.

"Right. Of course. You're right." She moved around him, shaky and disoriented.

They didn't look at each other for a time. Lola struggled for control, wanting to blurt out her feelings for him, knowing it wasn't the right time, knowing she didn't even know what she felt for him. Whatever it was; it was suffocating at the same time it was liberating.

It made her happy and sick. She was terrified and also giddy. Lola didn't even know if there were proper words to explain it all.

"I want you to understand—Sebastian and I are just friends," she said, her eyes zeroed in on his. His expression tightened before relaxing and he nodded. "You and me, we're not nothing. We are something. I'm not sure what, but it's...sort of epic." She smiled faintly, reaching for his hands. "I don't feel *obligated* to be around you. I feel happier because of you. I like being around you, all the time. I want you in my life, Jack, no matter where my life takes me."

He nodded again, swallowing thickly. He brought her hands to his mouth and brushed his lips across them. "Same." He smiled wryly. "I really am not good at talking about this kind of stuff. Just know that—everything you said—it's the same for me."

"Good." She blew out a noisy breath and looked up, catching a bird hopping from tree limb to tree limb.

"Only three more weeks."

She faced him. "Until?"

Jack swiped a hand through his hair. "Until I'm done with school."

Unease swept through her. There was a reason he was bringing this up. What happened when Jack was done with school? Would he move away? Would that be the end of them before they really even started? She had been ready to go, regardless of her feelings for him, and she couldn't expect him to do no less. If he needed to leave to protect his sister, then she would have to accept it and live with it. His safety and his sister's safety was more important than her feelings.

"What happens then?"

He wouldn't look at her. "I don't know. I've been thinking..."

The fact that he averted his eyes from hers told her that whatever it was, she didn't want to hear it. "Thinking?" She held her breath, waiting with dread.

"I don't want to be like my old man. I don't want to end up a loser drunk who works at a factory my whole life. But there's my sister too. I can't leave her with him." Jack squinted his eyes against the sunset, his features striking against the rose-colored hues. "I think...I want—I'm going to enroll at the community college in Lansing."

Lansing was a city about thirty minutes from Morgan Creek that was triple the size and had its own two-year college.

Her breath left her in a whoosh and dizzying relief crashed over her. She tossed her head back and laughed. She'd been so scared and for nothing. Although, the depth of her reaction to the thought of not being able to see Jack anymore worried her on some subconscious level.

The scowl on Jack's face quickly erased all mirth from her. "You don't think I can do it?"

Lola touched his face, tenderness weaving through her and showing in her smile. "Oh, Jack, I have nothing but faith in your ability to do anything you want to do. I just...I was worried you were going to say you were moving away or something."

"What? *No.* I'm not leaving you." As soon as the words left his mouth, he winced and looked away.

"Good. I couldn't bear the thought of not seeing you," she said softly.

They shared a long, heated look. Eventually he broke eye contact. "It's going to be hard. Going to school, working, taking care of Isabelle." He leaned against the rock. "I'm moving out of the house. So is Isabelle. She's going to stay with me."

Such burden for one person. But Lola thought him all the more amazing for his unwavering dedication to his sister. "Where?"

"My boss, Jared, has an apartment above the garage. It's small, but decent. He's going to pay me less to stay there, but I'll make it work. Isabelle is going to get a part-time job to help out. He told me

I could stay there for free, but I'm not going to take advantage of him. He's too good to me as it is."

"You're amazing, you know that?"

He avoided her eyes and hunched his shoulders. "Thanks." Jack cleared his throat and glanced at her, the barest of smiles curving his lips.

"When are you moving out?"

"As soon as school's out."

"And your dad? Does he know?"

His lips twisted. "No."

"Are you—"

He straightened. "I don't want to talk about him." The light was fading and his features were partly in shadow, giving him a predatory look. Funnily enough, she liked the look on him. It fit his personality—dark, arrogant, strong.

"Okay. But if you want to—"

He grinned. "I know. You'll listen."

"Yes. I'll listen."

He grabbed her face and pressed a hard kiss to her forehead. "Thanks. I have to get home. Isabelle's making me supper. She's horrible at it, but she tries."

Lola laughed. "I'd say enjoy the meal, but..."

"Yeah."

"Need a lift?"

He paused, shrugging. "Sure. If you promise not to play P!nk."

With a sigh, she said, "I promise."

CHAPTER 14

"THIS IS FOR YOU." A brown photo album was placed on the table before Lola. "I thought you might like to see these."

She set her mug of hot chocolate down and stared at the book. "Are they...?"

"Yes. Your father. Lots of pictures of your father. Your mother. And you."

Her eyes dampened and apprehension picked up her pulse. "Thank you," she told her aunt.

She'd only seen a handful of pictures of her dad and only then because she'd found them in a box. When Lola had approached her mom with them, she'd cried, so she put them back and never looked at them again in front of her mother. There were times, though, when Lana had opened up about her husband. Fleeting and far too sporadic, but each memory she'd shared with her had been a gift.

She shook herself back to the present. "What did you say?"

Blair, clad in pink and blue pajamas and hair upswept in a messy ponytail, smiled and ruffled up Lola's hair. "I said, you're very welcome. I'll be in my office working on an article if you need or want anything."

She absently righted her hair, her eyes intent on her aunt. "Do you have to? I mean, would you look at them with me?"

Her face softened and she nodded. "You bet I will. I didn't know if you'd want company or not." She pulled out a chair and sat down beside her, sipping her tea. "Go ahead," she urged when Lola continued to stare at the book.

On the first page was a photo of a gangly teenager with brown hair and brown eyes. He hadn't grown into his nose or chin yet. He was tall, thin, and posed like a ninja. She laughed, wiping at her wet eyes.

"He was quite the character, let me tell you."

Lola turned the page and saw a similar photograph. She waited for her aunt to elaborate.

"Joe was a goof. He had an infectious laugh. People liked him. He was funny, popular in school, handsome, athletic. There didn't seem to be anything he couldn't do. I wanted to be like him. Which is what made me pick up a camera. He was a great photographer. He knew how to capture a person's essence, you know? I have some of his work framed on the walls in my office. I'll show you sometime. Let you pick one out to keep."

She took a deep breath. "I'd like that. Thank you."

"I'm not saying my brother was perfect. He wasn't. He had a quick temper and could be overbearingly stubborn at times, but he felt strongly about things and stood up for what he thought was right." Blair smiled, lost in memories. "He was a good brother. Usually older siblings are mean and pick on the younger brother or sister, but not Joe. He always looked out for me. He stood up for me at school when other kids were bullying me." Her voice cracked and she cleared her throat. "He said he fell in love with your mom the instant he saw her. Did she ever tell you how they met?"

Lola shook her head, fascinated by the treasure being bestowed upon her. She didn't want to speak for fear of getting her aunt off track and missing something she would have told her had she not interrupted.

Blair took a drink of her tea and stared out the window with a thoughtful look on her face. "Lana was nineteen, Joe was twenty. It was wintertime and he was stopped at a set of stoplights. She rear-ended him." She laughed. "He said he got out of his car ready to do some yelling and then he looked at her and forget everything he was going to say. They were married less than a year later."

She rapidly blinked her eyes, hastily turning the page. A wedding picture of her mom and dad greeted her. They were looking at each other, each smiling. Her dad was in a black tuxedo and her mother in a frothy dress of white. They were beautiful, happy. Another page showed her father holding her as a baby, his face crinkled with joy. Lola was fat and bald and drooling.

"I don't understand how I can miss him so much when I don't even really remember him," she whispered.

"You were his world. He loved you so much," Blair said quietly.

An ache formed where her heart was. She sat back and lowered her head. "It's like I remember a ghost. I faintly remember a deep voice, a sense of contentment, strong arms. That's all I have of my dad." Her throat was tight as she tried to hold tears in.

"Don't be sad for not knowing him. Be glad he knew you, if only for a short time."

Her lower lip trembled. She wanted her dad. She wanted him back and alive and she wanted to erase everything, all the years, since his death. Lola wanted them to start over—her mother, father, and her. She wanted to *know* her dad. And she wanted her mother back too. She missed her. Lola couldn't believe how devastated she was by her mom's absence. She didn't want to know any of this, any of this pain and sadness and tragedy.

Lola wished she could go back in time—wished that all of them could. Her pain escalated when she thought of Jack and his life. She just wanted him okay. Lola wanted his mother back in his life and his father gone and he and his sister okay. She wanted him never to have been hit or yelled at or made to feel like he was nothing. She wanted him safe.

She wanted to close in on herself, to curl up in a ball and disappear. Tears streamed down her cheeks as she finally broke. She couldn't stop. It was too much. All of it was too much and Lola was cracking under the strain of holding it all together when all she wanted to do was lie down and never get up, never have to face any of this again.

"I want my mom back. I miss my mom. I just want my mom," she whispered.

"I know you do." Blair wrapped her arms around her and helped her to the floor, where she rocked her back and forth, caressing her hair and saying nothing. She clutched her aunt, needing to be comforted, needing to know someone cared. "Everything's going to be okay, I promise," her aunt told her in a soothing tone.

Lola desperately wanted to believe her.

IT WAS COLD AND RAINY out on the day she found herself outside her mother's house. The sky was gray, and everything was darker than usual. It fit somehow. She stood on the sidewalk, staring at the tan building that had been a haven at one time and then a prison. No lights shone from the inside. No black car took up the driveway space.

She shivered, her jacket protecting her from the dampness, but not the chill in the air. She didn't know why she was there. She supposed it was time to confront her mother, if she wanted to move on. She slowly walked to the front door, not sure if she knocked or just walked in. She decided to knock. When there was no answer after the third knock, she glanced over her shoulder, and seeing that no one was watching her, she tried the doorknob. It was locked.

Relief and disappointment hit her at the same time. Lola crouched beside a window and put her hands to it, trying to see inside. From what she could see in the darkened living room, it looked the same as it always had. She wasn't sure what she had expected to find—some visible sign of the tragedy that had taken place there, she supposed. Lola swallowed and moved through the wet grass to the side of the house, pausing next to her mother's bedroom window. Without warning, fear slammed into her and she sucked in a sharp breath, hurrying past the window. She stopped near her old room, a hand to the house, and hung her head.

Gathering her courage, she looked up and studied the window, wondering if it was still unlocked. Lola put her hands to the cool wet glass and pushed up. It opened, her pulse quickening as it slid up. Before she could change her mind, she maneuvered herself through the window and into her bedroom. The room was cool and musty smelling. She glanced around it, emotions strangling her the longer she stood there. Lola blinked her stinging eyes and moved on, into the hallway. The house seemed empty, disused. It was an eerie feeling and she found she didn't like it. It was unnatural.

Her heartbeat pounded and she had to keep reminding herself that Bob was locked up, that he wasn't there, and he couldn't harm her anymore. She stared at the closed door to her mother's bedroom, struggling to breathe. She didn't know what compulsion had her do what she did next—some form of morbid curiosity, maybe. It was as though she had to physically see that no harm resided on the other side of the door. Her hand shook as it closed around the doorknob and she slowly pushed the door open.

She exhaled deeply, her shoulders going limp. It was just an unoccupied room with a bed and dresser—but the things that had happened in it, the things that had almost happened in it, had added a darkness to it. The walls were stamped with a menacing quality; left there from the man who'd lived within them. Lola went through the rest of the house, not sure what she was searching for. Peace, maybe. Closure, definitely. She didn't find it. In fact, all she found was an empty house.

Her mother was gone.

LOLA FLUNG HER COAT DOWN by the door and kicked her shoes off, suspicion carrying her faster than her normal pace. Her mom couldn't have just vanished. *Someone* had to know where she was—Blair had to know. She had to, right? Why didn't she tell her? Did she move? Was she not coming back? Tears and hurt and anger propelled her forward. Where was her mom?

She stormed up the stairs to Blair's office. Her aunt sat at her desk, staring at a computer screen. Her hair was pulled back in a ponytail and she wore purple sweats. She turned when she sensed Lola behind her, frowning at her drowned appearance. "Everything okay?"

"Do you know where my mother is?"

She looked down, admitting her guilt without speaking a word.

"You knew she left and you didn't tell me? Where is she?"

"Lola, she didn't want you to know," Blair started.

"Where *is* she?" she demanded. She couldn't believe her aunt would keep such information from her. She'd been agonizing over her mother's absence, wondering why she'd stayed away, and she had known—all this time she'd known she was gone. She felt betrayed.

Her aunt got to her feet. "She's in a mental institution. Lana admitted herself the day after...after what happened to you. She's sick and she has been for a long time. Lana suffers from depression and it's gotten worse, gotten debilitating, since she married Bob. She's getting the help she needs, so she can be a mother to you again. She's doing this for you. She's doing this because she loves you."

Lola swayed on her feet, bumped into the doorframe and stayed there, allowing it to support her. She didn't know what she felt. She didn't know what she *should* feel. "Are you saying," she began in a voice that trembled, "that all this time I've been wondering why she's hasn't been to see me, she's been in some hospital? Why didn't she call me, or write? Why hasn't she contacted me in any way?"

"I don't know." She shrugged helplessly, sorrow etched into her features. "I only know what I was told." Blair crossed the room and grabbed her arms. "But I know she's doing it for you. She's there for you. She filed for divorce from Bob. I also was told the house will be going up for sale soon."

She stared at her aunt. "How do you know these things?"

"Social Services keeps in contact with her per her request and they relay the information on to me."

"You could have told me."

"It was Lana's wish that I not tell you. I don't know why. But…I wasn't going to lie to you if you asked me outright. I'm sorry."

Her mother loved her. She hadn't abandoned her. She was going to get help. She'd left Bob. Despondency washed away with her tears and was replaced with wonder. "I thought she stopped loving me. I thought she didn't want me anymore." She wiped her eyes. "I feel…relief, maybe? I don't know what I feel. Better somehow. Isn't that crazy?"

Blair kissed her forehead. "It would be crazy if you didn't. Come on, let's get some warm clothes on you and some hot chocolate into you."

SHE HAD GAINED SOME WEIGHT back. Her cheeks weren't so hollowed out; her ribs didn't stick out quite so far. Blair tried and tried, but she just couldn't cook. Lola had slowly taken that over and both of them were okay with it. Her food experiments still continued, and continued to fail as well, but it was fun to have something to do together. Lola's mom couldn't be replaced, flaws and all, but it was starting to not hurt quite so much when she thought of her. Blair had made a home for her, was her family, and took care of her, but she wasn't her mom. She ached to see her, to finally hug her without reservations, to have hope and forgiveness.

Piper and Larry slept with her every night—her two security blankets against the night and all the scary things it held for Lola. The fur balls eased her anxiety and made her feel a little safer. Snuggling with them was like having her own personal living, breathing stuffed animals. Maybe it was dumb, but it worked.

School was over in two weeks. Things were still unsteady and at times awkward with Sebastian and Rachel, who were dating, but she was working at it and her inclination to push others away was lessening. Roxanne had a meltdown when she saw them walking hand in hand down the hallway at school. She threw a book at a locker—the locker consequently dented and she had to pay for its repair, plus serve detention. That little detail had brought a faint smile to Lola's mouth.

She quickly dressed in jean shorts and a hot pink tank top, pulling her hair into a high ponytail. It was Saturday and Lola had the day off from work. Her plans consisted of doing nothing but relaxing and maybe writing a little. Wavy auburn wisps fell out of the ponytail to frame her face. She finally had no stitches to mar it, no bruises to discolor it. She smiled at her reflection in the bathroom and twirled out of the cerulean blue room.

She walked down the stairs and grabbed the folder full of her poetry from the coffee table. She walked into the kitchen, inhaling coffee and something banana-y. Blair was at the stove, flipping pancakes. Some were black, others runny. Not a single golden brown one was to be found.

"Banana pumpkin pancakes. Want to try one?" She didn't have a chance to answer when Blair said, "Yeah. Me either." She turned the burner off. "How about some toast with peanut butter and honey?"

She smiled. "Sounds great."

"At least I can make coffee," she mumbled to herself, scratching the butt of her purple pajama pants with a spatula caked in pancake batter.

Lola held in another smile, but it was hard. She poured herself a cup of coffee, carefully sipping it as she eyed her aunt's latest creation—or *mis*creation.

"What's on the agenda for today?"

"I thought I'd sit out back and write."

"Good idea! Mind if I join you? I seriously need to get some writing done before I get fired."

"They won't fire you. They love you. The cookies they sent last week said so. What's the topic this month?"

"They probably sent the cookies so my ward wouldn't starve." She winked. "The topic is boxers or briefs. I mean, really? You'd think there'd be something more worthwhile to interest women than what kind of underwear their men wear. Apparently not." Blair handed Lola a plate with toast on it. She looked down at her clothes and sighed. "I'll take a shower and meet you out back."

Juggling her coffee, plate, and folder in her arms, she went to the backyard. The sun was hot and she was glad she'd thought to put on sunscreen and sunglasses. Her pale skin had a slight glow to it from the fire in the sky and that was all the luminosity she wanted. Any quiet time turned her thoughts to Jack and today was no exception. Lola set her stuff down on the bench and took a cleansing breath of air. It was rare that she wasn't thinking of him, actually. He was fire to her soul and air to her lungs. That twist to his upper lip, his cocky attitude, the way his green eyes darkened on her—he made her pulse go crazy.

She opened the folder and stared at the depressing words that used to make up her life. She didn't want to write about that anymore. That was the old Lola, in her old life. It wasn't her anymore. She wanted to write about hope, about happiness, about *good* things. She wanted to write about Jack. With a smile on her lips, she brought the pen to paper. He said speaking about emotions was hard for him, but she also wasn't the greatest at it either—writing them had always been easier for her. If Lola couldn't tell him what he meant to her, maybe she could show him.

Safe And Sound
When I'm lost and can't find my way,
When the monsters are too close and I can't breathe,
When hope is gone and desolation threatens to drown me,
When I can't go on,
When I need someone to be there for me,
When I smile, when I cry, when I laugh,
When I'm consumed by emotions I don't understand,
When I love,
You're there—you're my safe and sound,
You're my safe and sound.

LOLA TURNED TO CLOSE FRONT the door, excited and nervous at the same time. She was going to tell Jack how she felt about him, finally. Or, at least, she was going to give him the poem and see how he reacted. Doubts pulled her toward the safety of the house, but she pushed them away. The way he looked at her, the way he talked to her and touched her—he had to feel the same. *Now or never, Lola.* She looked up and reared back, instantly wary. It was another scorcher of a day, but just the sight that greeted her was enough to make her go cold.

"Hi." Roxanne said, trying to smile and grimacing instead. She stood on the last step to the porch, posed as though about to flee, but stiff and unmoving, like she was forcing herself not to. Her fiery red hair was braided and she had on minimal makeup. She wore a plain white tee shirt and khaki shorts. To put it plainly—she looked nothing like herself.

Lola brushed hair damp with perspiration from her brow, her hand unconsciously crumpling the sheet of paper within it. She shoved it into her back pocket and met the girl's somber gaze. "You should go. I don't need any more stitches."

She looked away, her throat convulsing as she swallowed. "I'm really sorry about that," she said quietly. She hugged herself as she looked at Lola, as though gathering strength from her own embrace. "I acted without thinking. I tend to do that a lot." She inhaled audibly, adding, "You must hate me."

Studying her pale, forlorn features, she felt many things, but none of them were hate. Roxanne's treatment of her had been so insignificant compared to everything else going on in her life. She felt remorseful, more than anything. "No. I don't hate you. I feel bad for you."

Roxanne snorted. "That's so like you. You've always been a good person, even to those who don't deserve it. Like me. It's annoying, really." She wiped her eyes. "I'm sorry about the way I treated you. I had no idea what you were going through at home. Not that that matters. I shouldn't have been mean to you no matter what. Most of all, I'm sorry I lost someone I love…"

Her lower lip trembled and she bit it, blinking her eyes. "Because of my actions…because I was jealous of you and hurtful. I made it impossible for Sebastian to be with me. He's a decent guy and I should have realized he wouldn't put up with that kind of behavior for long. I just—I don't know—I didn't think. Like I said, I do that a lot, and now I have to live with the consequences of my actions." Tears trailed down her face, but Roxanne seemed uncaring of them as she kept eye contact with her. "I know I'm not worthy of it, not yet, but do you think maybe someday you'll be able to forgive me?"

Her heart twisted as she stared at the broken girl standing before her; strong enough to admit she'd wronged her and asking to be forgiven. Respect for her budded inside Lola and she moved for her. Not surprisingly, she flinched, but Lola lightly hugged her anyway. "I forgive you." She paused. "But I do need to even the score."

She pulled back, her face drawn in fright. "What?"

"Just kidding." Lola smirked.

"Oh." The relief on her face was comical. "Would you...do you think you'd...like to hang out sometime or something?"

"Now you're pushing it," she said with a smile.

"Yeah. I suppose I am. So...I guess I'll see you." She turned and headed down the street.

Lola watched her go, marveling at the way people could change. She was an expert on that. If she'd never met Jack, she wouldn't be the way she was. If events hadn't taken her in the direction they had, she never would have met him. It was strange how things worked out. She closed her eyes, her stomach swirling, and started her walk.

A FINE SHEEN OF SWEAT covered her skin by the time she reached their spot. Her throat was dry and she wished she would have thought to bring a bottle of water. Unruly locks of hair had fallen from her ponytail and were plastered to the sides of her face. Not exactly how she wanted to present herself, but it didn't matter because he wasn't there. A warm breeze fluttered her hair in her eyes and she absently pushed it away, examining the rock and surrounding trees.

She reached out a hand and ran her fingers along the jagged, smooth stone. How could an inanimate object hold so much meaning to her? This was the place where she'd been reborn, where Lola had found a reason to keep living. This was where she'd met Jack for the first time. A rueful smile turned her lips upward. She remembered him now. He'd been so defensive with his shoulders hunched, and the cruel words he'd spewed forth had allowed tears to flow more freely that had already desperately needed to. It was odd how it had actually been cathartic, in some twisted way.

She remembered how hemflinched when she began to cry, his eyes tragic and his features contorted with regret. His lip had been split, a bruise on his cheekbone. Jack's sorrow and anger had touched her in an unexplainable way—even as she'd cried for herself, some of them had been for the battered boy staring back at her. It was too bad she'd blocked pretty much everything about that day from her mind for months; she would have liked to have known him sooner. If only she could block out that last night in her mother's house from her mind as well.

Bob's court date was in two weeks.

She closed her eyes and took a shuddering breath, pressing her forehead against the stone, her heated flesh cooling against it. She spontaneously pulled herself up the rock, scraping her hands and knees in the process, and sat down. The sun beat against her back through the light material of her tank top. Lola pulled her knees to her chest and watched birds and squirrels navigate through the forest, finding solace in nature; the woodsy smell relaxing. She breathed deeply, in and out, as Blair had taught her through the yoga exercises they did together every other day.

It was hard to believe she only had one more school year left and she could leave Morgan Creek and all the bad memories. She swallowed, thinking of her mother. She had a lot of good memories of her too and she tried not to let the bad overshadow the good. Her mom's absence made it hard to think that way. She wanted to see her. Blair told her to let herself heal, to focus on herself for a while and no one else. She couldn't do it—she couldn't entirely heal until she had answers. There were so many things she didn't understand. There was Jack and his sister and their situation and all the intense emotions he made her feel. There was the fear of Bob that never completely left her. There was the pain in her chest each time she thought of her mom.

Her dreams, her life, *everything* had been put on pause this past year. Every day had been solely set on surviving, more mentally than physically. She shivered. He'd almost succeeded in the end—he'd almost broken her. Lola blinked her eyes and made herself think of better things, of her future. It was almost unimaginable to think of leaving Blair. They'd only just reconnected and a year didn't seem like enough time to get to know each other. It really wasn't. She was all she had of her father and his side of the family. Blair was the only living relative she had other than her mother.

Lola thought of starting at the community college in Lansing to get her generals done and then continuing on from there, maybe with a major in something with writing. Her aunt had told her she could live with her while she went to college and she was seriously considering it, but it wasn't anything she had to decide today. Today was the day she told Jack how she felt about him.

CHAPTER 15

HER FOOTSTEPS SLOWED THE CLOSER she got to the house. What if Jack wasn't there? What if his father *was*? She didn't think his dad would do anything to her, not physically anyway, but just knowing what he'd done to his son, and continued to do, was enough to make her loathe and fear him at the same time. He was a man like Bob Holden and 'man' was too good a word for him.

The air was stifling and Lola wiped her moist brow. The neglected white farmhouse loomed before her; the yard with all its many trees reminded her of their unofficial meeting spot. It was still and silent out, the sounds of nature all she heard. She took a deep breath, rounded up her nerve, and knocked on the door. Lola heard footsteps. Almost immediately, the door opened and there stood Isabelle in a purple and white striped shirt and white capris.

"Hi." She smiled. "How are you, Isabelle?"

Jack's sister held the door so Lola couldn't see past her, looking so much like her brother with her churlish expression that she blinked a few times in surprise. *Now* she could see the resemblance.

"He's not here." Something in her face gave Lola pause. Her eyes darted back and forth as she gnawed on her lower lip. She was scared.

"What's going on?" Lola asked in a low voice.

"Nothing," she answered quickly. "You should leave." She tried to shut the door and Lola put a hand out, stopping her.

"Jack's here, isn't he? Is he hurt?"

Isabelle's face crumpled and tears streamed down her face. She opened her mouth, but no words would come forth.

Panic slammed in Lola, jumpstarting her pulse. "Isabelle! Where *is* he? What happened?"

"Go away!" she wailed, pushing harder on the door.

Fear and adrenaline gave Lola strength and she shoved the door open so wide it banged against a chair. "I'm not leaving until I see him."

"He'll be back any minute. You can't *be* here! *Please.*" She clutched at her arm as Lola stormed into the house. Her resistance turned into clinging and Lola feared she was the only thing holding her up. "Jack wouldn't want you here. He wouldn't want you to see him," she whispered, her eyes luminous with unshed tears.

She went still as her eyes took in the empty vodka bottles on the counter, the shattered dishes on the kitchen floor, the smear of blood on the doorframe. Her throat tightened. *Oh, God, please let him be okay.*

"You have to go." Jack's sister clung to her, sobbing uncontrollably. "You have to go."

"I'm not leaving," she told her, "so I suggest you tell me where he is. *Now*. Before your dad gets back."

Isabelle nodded, her eyes wide, and pointed a shaking finger to the living room. "Upstairs. Second room. Please. *Help him.*"

I will, she silently vowed, sprinting for the stairs. She didn't think about consequences, she didn't think about what could happen if and when their dad showed up. Lola only thought of Jack. She had to get to him, she had to help him.

The second bedroom was dark and the metallic smell hit her as soon as she opened the door. Moments that altered you and defined you as who you were or who you came to be—seeing Jack like this was one of themt. It was like her heart stopped, her brain raced but formed no logical thought, and it was surreal. Her world changed in that instant.

She was aware of all she could lose.

Jack wasn't moving, his chest barely lifting with each shallow breath he took. Even in the dim light she could see his face was a myriad of bruises and swelling. She looked around the room, searching for a light switch. When she turned it on she almost wished she hadn't. Lola pressed a hand to her stomach, thinking she might vomit. His beautiful face was unrecognizable with cuts and blood. She wanted to touch him, but was scared she would hurt him even more.

"Jack?" she whispered, her voice cracking.

His eyelids fluttered, but didn't open. With a sinking sensation, she realized he couldn't—his eyes were swollen shut. "Shouldn't ... be ... here," he struggled to get out.

Lola began to cry. Again and again her hand went to touch him and she pulled it back. She sank onto her knees beside the bed. Even his hands were cut and bleeding, but she didn't know how much of that blood was from other wounds or if it was even his. A noise alerted her they weren't alone and she jerked her head to the side, posed protectively over Jack.

Isabelle hovered near the door, shaking and pale. She tried to speak and finally choked out, "He's never been this hard on him before."

"What *happened*?" she demanded, unable to take her eyes from Jack's wrecked face. He wore a shirt and shorts, and his legs were unaffected, but she didn't know about his upper body. He needed a doctor. They needed to get him somewhere so he could be properly checked out, and if he needed to be, cared for. She couldn't imagine all he had were superficial wounds.

"Jack told him about moving out. I thought...I thought he was going to kill him," she said, sinking to the floor and covering her face with her hands as she quietly wept.

Determination overtook Lola and she got to her feet. She allowed it in to wipe out the pain and fear, needing to be strong and focused. "Where's a phone?" Isabelle didn't answer, too lost in her own pain to hear her.

Lola knelt beside her and pushed her hands away from her face. "Look at me, Isabelle." She shook her head, trying to get away. She grabbed her shoulders and shook her. "*Look at me.*" Isabelle did then and something in Lola's expression quieted her. "I need a phone. Jack needs a doctor."

"No!" She shook her head. "He doesn't want a doctor."

Lola set her jaw and spoke slowly, "Your brother could have internal bleeding, wounds we don't even know about, *broken bones*. He needs a doctor."

"Jar...ed," was whispered raggedly from across the room.

Lola looked at her. "You know where Jared is?"

She nodded.

"Go get him. Now. *Now.*"

Isabelle shot to her feet and ran, her feet thundering against the floor in her haste.

Lola went to Jack, carefully brushing his hair back. Emotions welled up inside her, threatening to burst. A faint sob left her and Lola placed her hands over her face. The barest of touches against her hand had her lowering them. She stared down at Jack, hurting for him. She gently took his outstretched hand into hers and kissed the broken skin.

"I'm...okay."

She snorted, but it sounded choked. "Sure you are. You've never looked better, I can vouch for that."

She thought maybe he tried to smile, but it came out looking like a grimace. "You're here."

"I am."

"Then I'm okay," he told her again.

"HOW IS HE DOING?"

Lola started, sloshing hot coffee on her hand. She ran to the sink and turned on the cold water, holding her pink flesh under it.

"Sorry," Blair said. "I didn't mean to scare you."

She rubbed her face and leaned her hips against the counter, staring out the kitchen window at the gray cast sky. Lola was so tired. "It's fine. And he's okay, considering. He looks worse now than he did four days ago. Nothing broken, as far as we know." She set her coffee mug down and looked at her aunt, her self-control on the verge of shattering.

Blair pressed her lips together and reached for her. "Oh, honey, I'm so sorry."

There it went.

Lola sobbed, hanging onto her aunt just to stay upright. Blair hugged her tight, pressing a kiss to her temple. She moved away from her aunt's comforting arms, wiping her eyes. "This is so messed up. Really."

"He needs to press charges. And he should have gone to the doctor," she said for about the fiftieth time.

"He refuses to press charges. He's scared if he does anything more to anger his dad he'll lose his sister. And Dr. Jones looked him over at the apartment. It was the most Jack would agree to."

"Sebastian's mom will report it. It's her job to."

"She would, if any of us had told her the truth. He's eighteen, an adult. Jack said he fell and hit his face against a door. She didn't believe it, of course, but no matter how many times she tried to get him to tell her what really happened, that's all he would say. He's stubborn like that."

Her aunt sighed. "I'm sure she loved that. As far as Isabelle is concerned, technically, he isn't her guardian. His father can say she has to stay with him. Jack could fight it and probably win, but it wouldn't be a fun process for any of them."

"I know. We've talked about it. A lot. At least they're out of that house now." She walked to the window, watching the rain blanket the earth in water. "He's missed too much school to graduate. He'll have to take summer classes to get his diploma. Or get a G.E.D. later."

Blair poured herself a cup of coffee and blew on it. "How is this Jared guy treating him?"

A half-hearted smiled curved her lips. "He's wonderful. You should have seen the way he took care of Jack. He's bullish and set in his ways, but so sweet too. He's more of a father to him than his real father. He's rough around the edges, but a nice guy. I'm glad Jack has someone like him in his life."

"Me too. What are the plans for tonight? Think Jack and Isabelle would like to come over for dinner?"

She pursed her lips, not sure how to politely decline.

"I'll order pizza," Blair stated, laughing.

Lola smiled. "Sure. I'll call Jack after school. Speaking of which, I need to go."

"Take the car. I have stuff to do around here, so I won't need it."

"Thanks. See you later." She spontaneously kissed her aunt on the cheek, smiling when she laughed.

SEBASTIAN AND RACHEL FLAGGED LOLA down in the hallway at lunchtime. They were a striking couple; both attractive and well-dressed. They'd even color coordinated with black shirts and dark jeans. Probably that hadn't been on purpose.

"Hey, guys. What's up?" Lola eyed the glass doors that led to the outside word.

She'd planned on checking up on Jack during her half hour lunch break and their appearance was cutting into her time. Lola shook the car keys in her hand, waiting impatiently for them to catch up, but trying not to be obvious about it. It smelled like gym socks and sweat in the almost empty corridor, with posters on the walls boasting school spirit for the Morgan Creek Wolves in silver and black lettering.

Sebastian slung an arm around her shoulders and pulled her to him, his deodorant and cologne enveloping her. He smelled nice, but she preferred Jack's scent. "Where are you going to in such a hurry?"

"I need to check on Jack," she said, shifting her feet. She was posed for flight, itching to be on her way.

"How's he doing?" he asked.

"He's healing." Physically. Mentally Jack would forever carry the scars of his father's abuse.

Rachel made a sympathetic sound. "I can't believe he fell and hit his face like that. Poor guy."

"Yeah," was all she would say, aware Sebastian's knowing eyes were on her. She was sure his mother had filled him in on her suspicions.

"We should hang out tonight, maybe get a pizza and a movie or something. Have some fun. What do you say?" Rachel nudged her boyfriend. "Sebastian?"

"I can't. I gotta help my dad out at the shop, remember?"

"Oh. That's right. Another time?"

She appreciated the offer, she did, but all she really cared about at that moment was seeing Jack. "Yeah. Sure," she blurted. "We'll talk later."

"You still owe me a sleepover!" Rachel called after her. "And a proper introduction to your boy toy!"

Lola smiled and waved, jogging toward the door.

JARED SUMMERS' WAS A WEALTHY man. Maybe he wasn't rich in money, but it was blatant he was with land. He owned hundreds of sprawling acres of wooded and farmed land. His house was old and brown, three stories high, and sparsely furnished. It had a distinct smell to it, a scent Lola was sure most farmhouses acquired through the years, especially ones owned by bachelors—like hay, or freshly mowed grass.

He was in his early forties, tall and lean, with light brown hair and tanned skin. He had lines that fanned out at the corners of his turquoise blue eyes and lips that rarely smiled, but Jared was handsome in a hard, unrefined way, like Jack. He was a quiet man who grunted more than he spoke. He was also a decent, fair man. Lola had nothing but respect and gratitude for him.

She also had big plans for him—he just didn't know it.

If not for him, Jack would be an entirely different person. If not for Jared, he might have turned into a clone of his father. Jared had quietly intervened during an impressionable age for him, offered him work and a place to go to escape his life at home, and changed his life without even knowing it.

A brown garage matched the house in color and stood slightly away from it, equally old and lacking in furniture and decorative pieces. But there was one thing it contained that was priceless to Lola. Her breathing picked up as she parked the Cavalier, already visualizing his sweetly arrogant smile and piercing green eyes.

She slammed the car door shut and ran toward the garage, rain drizzling on her, making her hair and clothes damp. She tugged the hood of her burnt orange sweatshirt over her head as she knocked on the door to the left of the garage doors. The acrid smell of cow manure offended her nostrils and Lola scrunched her nose up. When a second knock didn't get a response, she pushed the door open. "Hello? Jack?" she called, walking up the narrow staircase to the living quarters.

When he didn't respond, she told herself maybe he was taking a nap—the cold, dreary day made the pull of slumber hard to resist. Lola fought her own yawn as she scanned the room for inhabitants. All of the rooms, and there weren't many, were kept neutral with tan walls and brown carpet. A small living room was to the left of the kitchen, a shabby red couch and a brown recliner its only furniture. There was a TV stand where a small television resided. Windows overlooked the barn and silo and other farm equipment Lola couldn't put a name to. The kitchen had brown linoleum, an avocado stove, off-white refrigerator, and a wobbly table with two chairs.

The scent of coffee lingered in the apartment, following her as she searched the two bedrooms and finding them both empty. Lola sat on Jack's bed, fingering the frayed green blanket. Other than a sketchbook and pencil lying on a worn nightstand, the room was almost completely barren of personal items, as though even here Jack didn't feel like he could really open up to show his real self—or as if he knew his stay here would be temporary. They were so much alike—how long did it take for her to start feeling like Blair's home wasalso hers and not just a place she was impermanently allowed to stay at?

She glanced at the clock. Where *was* he? She didn't think he would be helping Jared so soon after being injured. He was too sore and not healed enough to be doing farm work, hut he was a stubborn man so anything was possible.

But Jared's more stubborn. Even as she thought it, Lola jumped to her feet, intuition telling her something wasn't right. She raced down the stairs, tripping over her feet and falling the last few steps. She twisted her wrist in the process, wincing and holding it to her chest as she ran.

"Jared!" she shouted, rain plastering her hair to her face, seeping through her clothes and shoes. "Jared!" It blurred her surroundings, making her disoriented for an instant. Logic kicked in after a moment—of course he couldn't hear her over the reverberation of barn machinery.

She slipped in the grass, caught herself with her elbow against the hard ground, jarring the already injured arm, and scrambled back to her feet. Gravel crunched under her shoes as she moved. She told herself not to overreact, that there could be a sensible reason for Jack's absence, but she couldn't believe her own thoughts. She banged open the barn door, the smell and sight of cows repelling her—a farm girl she would never be.

It was dim in the building and it took her a moment to catch her bearings. She wanted to shout his name, but knew enough not to upset the animals. Lola stared at the cement walking slab in the middle of the cows, knowing that was the way to Jared. She took a deep breath, gathered her strength, and went in search of him, walking carefully straight. One false move would put her far too close to the massive beasts.

Lola found him at the far end of the barn, knelt beside a monstrous being. She didn't want to scare him or make any sudden movements to spook the cow. "Jared," she whispered in a hoarse voice. Her throat burned from her earlier yelling and his name came out rough.

Jared jumped, knocking his head against a metal bar and cursing. He turned said injured head to glare at her. "*What?*" he asked in a clipped tone.

She opened her mouth, but no words came out. What did she say? She didn't even know where Jack was, she just had a feeling it was somewhere detrimental to his well-being—like his father's. Would he be so reckless as to return to his house? Her insides stiffened with fear as the answer came to her. Yes, he would.

Something in her face must have alerted him all was not right. Jared's features twisted from annoyance to concern. "Jack?"

"I came...to check on him. He's...he's not here." Her teeth chattered together. She shivered from the cold and dread.

He got to his feet and slowly approached her. "What do you mean he's not here? Where is he?"

"I don't...I don't know."

He slammed his hands on his hips and swore. He closed his eyes, his lips formed into a tight line. He opened his eyes and met her gaze. "I think I know where he is." He stormed through the barn and she hurried to follow.

"Where?" she called, searching for his receding form in the rain as she stumbled over the uneven, wet ground after him.

Jared hopped into a huge black Dodge truck and looked down at her. "You stay here."

Lola grabbed the door when he moved to shut it. "*No*," she told him, determination clenching her jaw.

"I'm not arguing with you."

"So don't."

For one tense moment their eyes collided. Jared looked away first, sighing. "Get in. You're letting rain water into the truck."

She ran around the truck, grabbing it as she slipped in the grass, and quickly hauled herself into the vehicle before he could take off without her. It was a short drive, neither of them talking. She was too anxious for small talk and Jared didn't particularly like talking of any form.

When the truck stopped outside Jack's father's house, Lola looked at Jared. "How did you know he'd be here?"

A muscle ticked under his eye. "Oh, just a hunch. See that truck? That'd be mine."

An old red pickup was parked in the driveway—the one Jack usually drove. Dread propelled her from the vehicle.

Jared stopped walking to tell her, "You wait in the truck."

She stiffened her spine and looked him in the eye, not even bothering to speak. She would not be left outside while whatever was going on inside. She needed to be with Jack, no matter what. Jared finally just sighed and shook his head, muttering something under his breath as they strode for the house.

A crash sounded from inside as they reached the door. Jared took off at a sprint and she was right behind him. The sight that greeted stopped her short. The kitchen table was broken down the middle, two uneven halves on the floor. Papers littered the floor, as though a hand had swiped them off a counter or table. It smelled like sweat and blood and...fear.

Jared stood in the doorway to the living room, not moving.

There was a grunt, a sickening cracking sound.

"Jared—" He raised a hand, not looking at her, and the words died on her lips. What was he looking at? What was on the other side of him? Lola didn't want to know, didn't want to see, but found her feet moving regardless.

It happened in slow motion, but so very quickly as well. There was a body, a man over the body, and blood—in streaks and smears over both of them. It felt like she was watching a movie—a horror movie that couldn't be real, but was. She gasped, putting a hand to her mouth. Nausea swirled in her stomach. At first she thought it was Jack on the floor and it took a minute to sink in that he was on top. The relief was palpable, dizzying, but then immediately replaced with dismay. Jack was okay, but he also wasn't—that was clear from his actions. Jack was straddling who she could only assume was his father's limp form, pummeling his face. The man was large, larger than Lola could have imagined, and yet he wasn't fighting back. Why wasn't he fighting back?

She grabbed Jared's arm and squeezed. "Jared, stop him. You have to stop him!"

"He needs to do this," was the low reply.

"He's going to *kill* him." She didn't care about Jack's father, a man he'd never even deemed important enough to name in front of Lola, but he wouldn't be able to live with himself if he murdered a man, however horrible that person was. It would eat him up inside like a slow disease—it would turn him into someone he didn't want to be.

"This is for Isabelle. This is for *me*," Jack vehemently declared, landing another punch to a face that no longer looked like a face. The sound of flesh hitting flesh turned her stomach and she fought to keep her eyes on the scene. Looking away would make it seem like Jack was wrong, and although she didn't know if this was the correct way to handle the abuse brought on by that man's hands, she also knew to Jack, this *was* the right way.

Jared crouched beside Jack, reaching for him. "That's enough."

He shook him off, not even looking at him. "It's not enough. It'll never be enough," he muttered.

Lola watched Jack be consumed with hate; saw him losing himself, and reacted. She had to save him. He'd saved her. She had to reach him somehow. "Jack," she whispered, kneeling beside him. She ignored the unconscious man trapped under him, refusing to look at him.

He paused then, turning his head. His eyes blazed with vengeance, an unholy gleam lightening them to pale green. His face was different shades of yellow and purple—artwork in the form of bruises. His chest heaved up and down, up and down, as he crouched there, looking at her but not really *seeing* her. He looked scary, beautiful, like an avenging angel.

Her throat choked up. "*Jack.* There's something I want to tell you." She reached a hand out and touched a fresh cut on his already battered face. "I want you to know that...I love you." She wasn't sure of the depth of that love, she wasn't sure if it would be forever or fleeting, but she knew it was there. She loved him, and even if one day they were once again strangers, she would still have him in her heart.

Jack's eyes cleared and it was him again. "I hate him, Lola."

"I know you do," she told him, gently touching his sweat dampened brow.

His shoulders slumped forward as he hung his head. He got off the man and, on his knees, proud and unremorseful, he faced Lola. She was vaguely aware of Jared moving the man none too gently and looking him over to check the extent of his wounds. She reached for him and held his head against her chest. His arms slowly raised, his hands barely touching her, as though afraid she would disappear if he held her too close. Then Jack crushed her to him, something wet and warm dripping down her skin. It was tears. He was crying. Her lips trembled and she pressed them tightly together to halt it. She put her chin against his soft hair, her own grief quietly falling down her cheeks.

Jared caught her eye, motioned that he would be outside. She jerked her head in acknowledgement.

"You're not alone. Don't ever feel like you're alone. I'm here. I'm here for you," she whispered brokenly.

Jack didn't respond, but his grip on her tightened, his arms fully cocooning her to him, telling her without words that he needed her to be there for him.

CHAPTER 16

"I DON'T HAVE TO TELL you that was stupid."

Jack sat on the couch, watching Jared pace before him. Lola sat beside him, an arm around his waist. She was thinking the same thing, but didn't necessarily agree that right now was the time to discuss it.

"And yet you just did."

She gave him a slight squeeze in warning. Jared was stopped in front of him, signature scowl in place. The two of them were like firecrackers when they arguing—one little spark and they both went off. "Nobody likes a smartass. He can press charges against you. You're eighteen. Then what? Then you lose Isabelle anyway."

It was true. Lola had thought the same thing just moments ago.

Jack shot to his feet, as tall and rangy as Jared. "I had to do it. For my peace of mind."

"You had to beat the crap out of your dad for your peace of mind?"

"*Yes*. I felt helpless, unable to fight for myself and Isabelle, unable to protect us. It was killing me, tearing me up inside." He strode to the window, keeping his back to them. His shoulders were tense, his hands in fists at his sides. Lola watched as his back muscles contracted under the thin black shirt he wore. "I had to do something. And I'm glad I did. Now he knows what I felt all those times he raised his hand to me."

She understood. Sometimes all you had left was the fight within yourself, the fight to survive, whatever it took. Sometimes you had to seek your own form of justice in order to move on.

"He won't go to the police. He won't fight me getting guardianship over Isabelle. We won't ever see him again." His words were firm and spoken with conviction.

"How do you know that?" she asked, wanting it to be true.

He spun around, pinning her with his heated gaze. "Because I told him if he did, I'd air all his dirty little secrets. I'd tell the entire world about the years of abuse. He knows I meant it. He's scared. And a coward. He won't talk."

"I hope you're right," Jared said.

"I am."

They stared at each other for a long moment. Jared finally nodded. "Okay. I gotta get back to my chores." He turned to Lola. "Shouldn't you be getting back to school?"

She jumped up. "Um, yeah, I should." She walked over to Jack and gently touched his bruised cheek. "I'm so proud of you," she told him quietly.

He inhaled deeply and turned his cheek into her palm, closing his eyes. "For what?"

"For being you."

He swallowed and moved away, eyeing the curtain as though the drab fabric was somehow fascinating.

She knew it was time to change the subject. "My aunt invited you and Isabelle over for supper. She's getting pizzas," she was quick to add at Jack's look. She'd told him all about Blair's bad luck in the kitchen. "And you," she said with a pointed look at Jared. Blair hadn't *not* invited him.

He froze at the top of the stairs. "Me?"

"Yep. We'll see you *all* at six." She didn't wait for an answer. Jared still hadn't moved by the time she got to the stairs, looking shell-shocked, so she just brushed past him.

IT WAS FUNNY HOW A memory had certain feelings and smells. Memories of her mom were always tinged in sadness; even as a child when Lola hadn't been able to understand, she'd still felt it. The time with Bob in her life was clouded with darkness. It was cloaked in fear, anger, hatred, helplessness.

But this time, with Jack, it was *beautiful*. It was sunshine and warmth, flowers and his seductive cologne. It was intense and frightening, overwhelming. It was happiness and love, but so much more than love too. She was healing, slowly but steadily, and he was a large part of the reason why. He had been away from his father for close to a week now and was healing in his own way too. He smiled and laughed more, held his shoulders a little straighter and his head a little higher. Years had been stripped from his face with the burden of his father gone.

Lola was lying on her bed beside him, staring at his face, taking in each detail. Even the small scars, the healing bruises and cuts, didn't detract from his beauty. If anything, they added to it. Those green eyes saw everything about her and still wanted her. Those cynical lips turned up for her alone. "What's it like at the apartment? Are things going okay?"

"Yeah. For the most part. Isabelle loves it. She has newfound freedom. She's enjoying herself a little *too* much."

She didn't doubt it. "What about you?"

"Not having my dad around is...I feel tremendous relief. Jared comes over every night to check up on us. I'm not used to that. But it's kind of nice, you know? Having someone look out for me. Of course, I guess he always kind of has. Do you know what he's charging me for rent?"

Lola shook her head.

"Fifty dollars—a *month*. And when I told him that wasn't nearly enough, he threatened to kick me out and fire me. He would too."

Respect for Jared went up a notch, although it was already pretty high. That man oozed integrity.

"You know what I think about the most, out of everything?" He didn't wait for her to respond. "Not about what my dad did to me, but that he could do it to someone else. *That's* what bothers me the most."

"You can report him."

"No. I just want to forget, I want it over with. Besides, I told him I'd be watching him and if I ever found out he hurt anyone else, I wouldn't stop until he was dead."

Alarmed, she said, "Jack."

"I wouldn't really," he said, smiling. "But he had to believe I meant it. He's a coward and a drunk and now he's scared. I don't want to talk about him anymore. I have better things to think about."

He trailed a calloused finger along her brow, down her nose, and stopped at her lips. Lola kissed his finger and he unconsciously shuddered. He leaned over and gave her a lingering kiss, touching his cheek to hers when they pulled apart. Lola was consumed by her feelings for him. When she thought of him she smiled, when he was near she was lighter, happier. Every minute of every day she wasn't with him, she missed him. Sometimes, even when he was with her, she still missed him.

"I can't believe your aunt allowed me up here."

"Well, the door *is* open."

"And she's right down the hall."

"I can't believe she and Jared actually hit it off and are going on a date."

Jack turned to his side, a knowing light in his eyes. "Yeah, because you didn't have anything to do with that."

Lola smiled. "I just got them together. The rest was up to them."

"Isabelle is happy you did that. She likes your aunt a lot."

"But not me."

"Not true. She's just overprotective of her big brother. I've always looked out for her; she's just doing the same."

Lola knew that and commended Isabelle greatly for it. She had spunk, that was for sure. "I suppose she didn't glare at me so much the last time I saw her," she grudgingly supplied, grinning when Jack laughed.

She loved his laugh. It was a beautiful sound, deep and rumbly. His eyes twinkled and she always fought not to kiss the mirth from his lips when it overtook him. It was priceless—each laugh a small treasure to behold. Lola took a deep breath and sat up. There was something she had to do, something she had been putting off.

"What?" he asked when she stared at him.

"I have something for you."

Jack sat up as well, touching her cheek. "Why do you look so terrified at the thought of giving it to me, whatever it is?"

She got down from the bed and opened the chest at the foot of it, taking her folder out. She opened it with fingers that trembled, swallowed, and pulled a sheet of paper from it. Without speaking, she handed it to him. Jack frowned at her, glancing down. As he read, his features transformed into that expressionless mask that gave so much away and she wondered what Jack thought of the words he was reading.

She fiddled with bottles of body spray on the dresser top as he read, gnawing on the inside of her bottom lip. Lola picked up the vanilla scented one and sniffed it, replacing the cap. What if he didn't like it? She pulled the cream curtain back and looked at the large tree in the front yard, studying the leaves. What if he thought it was stupid? Her pulse was thrumming an erratic beat in her wrists, the wait unbearable to her nerves.

Lola heard him move, felt him behind her. Her stomach flip-flopped. His hands warmed her shoulders and his breath tickled the sensitive skin under her ear. "Do you know what I love about you the most?" he whispered, causing her to shiver.

She wordlessly shook her head.

"How you manage to look past the bad and find the good—even with me. You looked past what I showed the world and wrecked me, but in a good way," he added when she stiffened. "You ruined me from turning into something I didn't want to be. I don't know how to show you how much you mean to me. You filled a hole in me."

She swallowed, her eyes welling with tears.

"Thank you for seeing the real me," he said with feeling, turning her around and showing her with his lips, with the passion of his kiss, what she meant to him.

SEBASTIAN'S BIRTHDAY AND GRADUATION PARTY were on the same day, at the end of May—it was double the festivities. Lola had reservations about being there, but only because her former residence was right across the street. She looked at her shimmering pink strapless dress in the mirror above her dresser and touched her upswept hair. Silver sandals glimmered on her feet, sparkling when the light caught them. Lola felt pretty.

Blair and she had gone dress shopping specifically for the occasion and treated themselves to manicures, pedicures, and haircuts and 'dos. Lola couldn't remember the last time she'd done something so fun, but as always, it had been darkened by the knowledge it wasn't her mother with her. She spritzed herself with lemon vanilla body spray and put sparkly earrings on. She smoothed her dress, feeling like a princess, or like she was going to prom. Lola hadn't gone this past year; she had had no reason to. She'd actually forgotten about it, its importance fading with her life in turmoil as it had been.

Next year, she promised herself. Her senior year would have to make up for her junior.

A knock sounded at the closed door. "Lola? Ready, honey?"

"Come in."

She turned, strangely nervous about revealing her appearance, and took in her aunt's look of awe. "Wow. You look...you look so beautiful. You got all the good parts of your mother and father."

She blushed, pleased with the compliment. "So do you. Jared's going to be drooling all over you."

"He better." Her aunt wore a teal off the shoulder dress and black heels. Her auburn hair was pinned to the side with a glittering black clip.

The closer it got to the time to leave, the more anxious she became. She felt bad that she wasn't looking forward to it, but she just kept thinking of the dark house across the street; its existence a taint on the happy occasion. She owed it to her friend to be there for him, she knew that. Lola paced the length of the living room, glancing out the window every few minutes.

"I can't do this," she said, closing her eyes. For some reason, the thought of seeing her old house in daylight was scarier than when she'd seen it under the gloom of clouds.

"Do what?"

She spun around and sucked in a sharp breath. Jack stood inside the doorway, wearing khaki shorts, a blue and white buttoned down shirt, and brown sandals. His clothing was nothing especially spectacular or noteworthy, but at the same time it was. Every time Lola saw him was like the first time she realized she was in love with him. Jack stared at her, not speaking, his eyes going up, then down, the length of her. His expression went blank, but when he raised his head his eyes smoldered. She felt faint, struggling to swallow.

"I'll just...be outside," Blair said and left.

"You cut your hair."

His ebony locks had been shorn and were now styled in messy disarray that looked good. Jack's eyes were greener somehow, his eyelashes thicker and longer without the hair hiding them. His features were sharper and breathtakingly gorgeous. Not a single bruise lingered on his face, not a cut or scrape marred it. There was nothing to take away from the beauty of his features. Lola felt a smile curve her lips. He no longer had a reason to hide, and in the cutting of his hair, he realized that.

"Had to make myself presentable." He took a step into the living room, and another.

"I like it."

He cocked his head, studying her.

Lola clasped her hands in front of her, self-conscious with his electric gaze on her. Those eyes didn't miss a thing, not one fine detail. Was it the artist in Jack that allowed him to see so much in a person, to look past the exterior and into the person's soul, to *know* her with just a glance? Or was it because it was him, and it was her, and no other reason? They were connected, inexplicably, by their lives, but also by their feelings for one another.

Jack stopped before her and Lola had to crane her head back to meet his gaze. He lifted a hand and trailed it down her cheek. "So soft," he murmured. Lola inhaled his scent she loved so much, closing her eyes. He dipped his head into the crevice between her shoulder and neck, his breath causing shivers down her arms. "You smell so good." She trembled, each nerve-ending on alert. "You look beautiful."

Jack lifted his head, cupped her face between his hands, and kissed her. Her stomach dipped and fluttered. It was a soft, slow kiss, full of tenderness. Lola opened her eyes and saw the green depths of his focused on her with such intensity, such longing. A throat cleared behind them and they pulled apart.

"Hate to break it up, but we gotta go." Jared leaned against the doorframe with his arms crossed. He wore jeans, a brown polo shirt, and boots.

"Jared! You dressed up," Lola teased, grabbing Jack's hand as they walked.

"Yeah, well, don't get used to it," he grumbled, heading out before them.

It was warm out, but there was a nice breeze to calm the temperature. Lola smelled flowers and sunshine, smiling at the summer day. It was too beautiful a day to ruin it with ghosts from the past. She straightened her back, her resolve returning. *You can do this. Be strong.*

When they got to the porch, Jack pulled her back and Lola looked at him in question. "What were you talking about when I got here, about not being able to do something?"

She looked to where Blair and Jared waited for them by her aunt's car. "Seeing my old house. It just...it's upsetting. It's silly, I know."

"No. It's not silly at all. Don't minimize your fears. But..." He put an arm around her and hugged her to him as they walked. "The house didn't hurt you. The people inside it did. Just remember that."

"And what about my mom?"

Jack gave her a fierce look. "Your mother gave up the best thing she had in her life. I know you miss her, I know you're confused and have all sorts of questions for her. But you're *better* than her, you're better than all of this. *She* wronged you, not the other way around. You didn't do anything wrong. You didn't deserve what happened to you. She's the one that needs to feel bad, not you.

"Sometimes there are no answers. You have to accept that. Maybe you'll never know what you think you need to know, but do you *really* need to know all the details, really? You know she wasn't there when you needed her, she *still* isn't here when you need her, but look around." Jack opened his arms wide. "You got me. You got your aunt. Jared. Sebastian. Rachel. Even Isabelle. You need to realize that and move on, as best you can. *I* had to realize that myself. When you let go of the pain and hurt and unanswered questions, *then* you'll be okay. You're safe now." He pressed a kiss to her forehead. "You're safe now. Remember that. *Believe* that."

Lola couldn't move, couldn't speak. She was stunned by his words, stunned by how very true they were. Her heart pounded as they sank in, melting warmth trickling through her. "You're so smart," she finally said, breathless.

Jack laughed.

"Can you, like, write that down for me so I can remind myself daily?"

He tapped his head. "It's all up here, even if only subconsciously. You won't forget." He propelled her toward the car.

THE PARTY WAS DYING DOWN as the sun set. The Jones' backyard had been turned into a celebratory palace, complete with a dance floor and DJ. Black and silver streamers littered chairs, tables, and the large canopy the tables and chairs sat under. Citronella candles marginally helped to keep the mosquitos at bay.

Sebastian had decided to wait until the party was over to open gifts. Lola was glad. The pile was *huge*. But hers she needed him to open before she left. She sat at a table by herself, watching her best friend and her boyfriend. They were talking across the backyard, Jack's eyes on her. They appeared to be getting along so she didn't want to interrupt them. Lola smiled when he winked at her.

The house had just been that—a house. Same as last time. Lola had stared at it for a minute, feeling emptiness more than anything, and turned away before stronger emotions had a chance to override her newfound acceptance.

"I love your boyfriend," Blair announced, sitting down beside Lola with a plate of cake in her hand. She offered a second plate to her, but she shook her head. Her aunt shrugged and ate from both plates.

"Really? Why?"

"*Yes*, really. Everything he said to you before we left, all those awesome words that came from his magnificent brain, were all things I was thinking and didn't know how to put into words. He's a *genius*. This cake is *so* good."

"Have you been drinking?"

She squinted one eye and measured with her fingers. "Little bit."

Jared appeared behind her chair. He watched her eat her two pieces of cake, a strange expression on his face. It took a moment for Lola to realize it was something like wonder. She turned her head to hide a smile.

"Hi, Jared! Want some cake? Oh. It's gone. Sorry. I'm tired." Her head fell back against Jared as her eyes closed, her body almost immediately going limp.

She stared at her aunt. "Did she just pass out?"

"She only had two glasses of wine." He had his hands on her shoulders, keeping her upright.

Lola laughed at the look on his face. It was a mix between incredibility and disgruntlement.

Jared's lips twitched as their eyes met. "Should probably take her home."

"Good idea. I just need Sebastian to open my gift and then we can go."

"We'll be in the car."

Jack rushed over as Jared hefted Blair's slack form into his arms. "What happened? Is she okay?"

"Oh, yeah. She's fine. Just drunk," he said dryly and maneuvered his way through the dispersing crowd.

Jack turned to her. "How did that happen?"

"He said she had two glasses of wine."

"Two? *Two?*"

Lola shrugged. She didn't understand it either. "I have to get Sebastian to open my present quick before we go. Coming?"

He hung back. "No. You go."

She frowned. "Why don't you want to go?"

"I don't want to intrude."

"You're not intruding."

"Lola." Jack gave her a look. "*Go.* It's okay for you to be with your best friend without me hovering. Sebastian said Rachel has big double dating plans so I'll go find out the details."

"That sounds like torture."

He kissed her forehead. "The things I do for you."

She weaved her way through people, stopping to give her goodbyes to Dr. Jones and Derek, both of whom hugged her tight and invited her over for supper the next week. Sebastian stood off to the side, watching his family and friends enjoy his party. His hands were shoved into the pockets of khaki pants, a white dress shirt tight against his muscular chest. His hair was slicked back, making his features more prominent. She watched him for a moment, emotions tightening her throat. Her childhood friend was a young man now. Bittersweet tenderness swept through her. He would be leaving soon, going to college in Iowa.

True, they had both changed and were different from a year ago, but some things, the most important things, never changed. He'd always been there for her, even when she hadn't known it, even when she hadn't wanted him to be. If he hadn't been there that last night, who knew what she would be like at this very moment, where she would be, *what* she would be.

Sebastian looked up, caught her eye, and grinned. Lola hurried to him, missing him already. She felt like crying. In fact, she was. She grabbed him and pulled him into a tight hug, his arms moving to hug her just as tightly.

"You're my best friend. Even if I get another best friend someday, you'll still always be the *best* best friend." Lola pulled away and wiped her eyes.

He swallowed, his eyes red. "You too. Always."

She laughed through her tears; wishing things didn't have to change. But that was life and that was the one constant, the one thing that never changed—things always changed.

"You have to open my present before I go."

"Okay."

"I'm going now," she told him when he didn't move.

"Oh." He straightened. "Where is it?"

She dashed a hand across her wet eyes and grabbed the present from the table of them, offering it to him.

Sebastian looked at the gift wrapped in blue paper, holding it in his hands. "Whatever it is, I'll love it just because it's from you."

"I know that. Open it."

He began to tear at the paper.

"It seems insignificant, but it's really something you always need, something you never want to lose," she told him.

He paused, understanding the significance of the gift. He lifted the lid from the box and reached in, pulling out an 8 X 10 canvas. Colors swirled together, different shades of blues and greens and purples melding, interlocking, becoming one. Four black letters stood out, bold and unable to ignore.

"I made this at a time when I had none, or at least, not much."

He kept his head down, tracing the four letters with his fingertip. It read: HOPE. He took a deep breath, wiped his eyes on his sleeve, and gave her a sweet smile. "This is the best gift I've ever gotten."

She patted his back. "I know." They shared a smile, laughing.

LOLA SAT STILL AS ISABELLE braided her hair, trying not to wince when she pulled it. She wasn't entirely sure it wasn't on purpose, so she said nothing. She didn't want to give her the satisfaction. They were in the living room of Blair's house, watching 'The Golden Girls' which just happened to be both of their favorite television shows of all time. It was too bad they didn't get along since they had so much in common. A half-eaten plate of chocolate chip cookies they'd baked together sat on the coffee table and two glasses of partially drunk milk beside it.

Jack had told Lola she'd somehow become Isabelle's role model, which was scary at best. Plus she didn't believe him. She thought she just hung around her to agitate her and she was *good* at it. It was turning into a weekly routine for Isabelle to show up at Lola's whenever Jack was working and Lola wasn't. If she didn't find her so amusing, she would have forbade her to come over a long time ago. Well, she told herself that anyway. Lola had to admit, grudgingly, that she enjoyed her company, sulky disposition and all.

"I can't do this!" Isabelle wailed and undid Lola's hair, being particularly rough as she shook it loose with her hand, her nails like talons in her thick hair.

"Hey. Easy! That's *real* hair on a *real* head, you know," she complained, ducking out of her reach. She moved from the floor to the bay window, putting plenty of space between them.

Her pretty face was set in a scowl, her arms crossed. "I *suck*. I'm never going to learn how to do this."

"You're never going to learn if you give up and throw fits," Lola said, rubbing her sore head.

"I do *not* throw fits!"

She looked at her, trying to find some patience. Isabelle had on a pretty pale green sundress and sandals, her blonde curls framing her face. The girl had no idea how pretty she was, even with a pout on her face—which was probably a good thing.

"Here. Grab that mirror and watch how I do it. Sit on the floor." Lola moved to the couch and sat behind her, parting her hair in threes. "I'll show you how to do it and then you can practice some more."

She was quiet as Lola worked, a look of concentration on her face as she watched her fingers move through her curls.

"May I ask why it is so important you learn to braid hair?"

She didn't answer, instead asking, "Who taught you how to braid hair?"

Their gazes collided in the handheld mirror. "My mother." Discomfort pricked her chest, but it wasn't the stabbing agony it used to be.

Isabelle looked down. "I didn't know my mom. She died when I was born. I never got to do any of those mother daughter things, like braiding hair. Jack tried." A warm smile stretched her lips. "He was terrible at it. My hair ended up in ratted knots that had to be cut out."

She laughed softly. "At least he tried, I guess."

"Yeah." She got a distant look on her face. "He's done so much for me, given up so much. I didn't really have a mother or father, just Jack. He was both. He was everything for me. He still is."

Lola quietly put a rubber band around the end of the braid. "There you go."

She put the mirror down and twisted to face her. "Thank you."

Uncomfortable and unused to the more sensitive side of Isabelle, Lola just nodded and got up to grab another cookie.

"My dad moved away."

She froze with the cookie halfway to her mouth, swallowing what was in her mouth. "Oh?"

Jack had told her, but it was another thing entirely for his sister to confide in her. For whatever reason, Isabelle had picked her as a confidant. Maybe she just had no one else to talk to—or maybe she knew she would understand.

Isabelle got to her feet and moved to the picture window, looking out at the sunny day. "I'm glad."

I am so glad.

Jack had been right. His father had signed over guardianship to him without qualm.

She turned to face Lola, studying her. "I'm also glad Jack has you. You're good for him. He deserves to be happy for once."

"He deserves to be happy for the rest of his life."

"So we're in agreement."

She shifted her feet, hating to admit it. "You could say that."

"Scary."

"You could say that too." Lola smiled when Isabelle laughed and spontaneously hugged her.

IT WAS A SUNNY DAY in early June when Lola got the news. She and her aunt were weeding the flowers around the house. It was dirty, time-consuming work, but it was also cathartic. It was hot out and Lola's top and shorts clung to her with sweat. The tree shade helped protect them from the sun, but not so much the heat. The lady from Social Services, Alice Jones, met them at the sidewalk with a somber expression. Her blonde hair was pinned back, her black glasses and white skirt jacket suit giving her a professional look.

Just like that Lola was shivering, her breaths coming out ragged and quick. Today was the day the judge made a decision about Bob. She both dreaded and eagerly anticipated the outcome.

"Hello, Lola. Blair."

Her aunt pulled off her gardening gloves and put a hand on her back, offering silent support.

"Hi," Lola barely got out.

"I have news."

She wanted to blurt out to get on with it, but manners kept her quiet, though she was sure an impatient expression was on her face. That she couldn't help. And then Alice spoke. Bob had been sentenced to ten years in prison, with possible parole after five. She stood there, not sure how to feel. She wasn't happy or sad or upset. She just felt relief. It was over. It was finally over.

Alice said a few more things, shook her hand, and went on her way. Lola stood there, staring at the spot she had been moments ago.

"Are you okay, Lola?"

"I...don't know. I don't really feel anything." Her eyes met her aunt's. "Is that normal?"

She smiled softly and brushed hair from her face. "Whatever you feel is normal."

SHE KEPT THINKING OF HER mother—that was what plagued her more than anything and kept her from completely healing. Most of the time, she was okay. Most of the time, Lola didn't think of her. But sometimes, when she did, she was struck motionless with pain. Other times it wasn't so bad.

Times like this, when she was alone, were the worst. That's when all the questions and doubts came forth and threatened to overwhelm her—when the sense of betrayal and numbing fear became too much. Lola's emotions were so conflicted. If she just knew. If she just knew *why* maybe she'd finally be able to put it behind her for good. She missed her. She wondered how she was doing. She wondered when she would see her again and what she would say when she did, and most especially, what she would feel.

She sat on her bed, staring at the framed 4 X 6 photograph. It was of her and her mother, taken by her father when she was two. Blair had given it to her—a piece of her father was now in her possession. He'd looked at this picture, he'd touched it. She brought it to her lips and kissed the cool glass. Her eyes were fixed on the image, the way her mother's blue eyes sparkled with life, the way she hugged Lola to her. In the picture she was looking at Lana, her profile in view, mouth open as she laughed. A tear fell from her eye, dropped to her mother's face, and blurred it.

She wanted nothing more than to see Jack, to have his arms around her. But he was at summer school, working on getting his G.E.D. and when he was done there, he had to work. Lola was alone to deal with her sorrow. Maybe that was the way it had to be. A memory tickled her mind and fought to the surface. She sat still, letting it take over. It was of her mother, holding Lola in her arms, rocking her and caressing her hair. She closed her eyes, inhaling a scent long forgotten and close to her heart. Cookies and cake and love—an imprint of safety and security followed it.

Mom.

A haunting melody swept over her, the voice soft and sure. Lola recognized the song as 'Brahms Lullaby'. A sense of awe curled within her stomach and tingled her scalp. She opened her eyes and took a deep breath, feeling something like peace hum through her. Her mom used to sing to her when she was sad or troubled—that was what she needed to associate her childhood with. *That* was the proof she needed to hang on to that her mother loved her. Infinite melancholy washed over her, but it was also cleansing. Finally, she had something to hang on to; a piece of the mother from her childhood she'd known existed.

One day, she would get the answers she sought—or maybe she wouldn't. Sometimes there were no answers, just like Jack had said.

For now, though, she simply had to have faith. It would have to be enough. She would heal. In time.

Lola smiled. She was going to be okay.

ABOUT THE AUTHOR:

Lindy Zart has been writing since she was a child. Luckily for readers, her writing has improved since then. She lives in Wisconsin with her husband, two sons, and one cat. Lindy loves hearing from people who enjoy her work.

You can connect with her online at:
https://twitter.com/LindyZart
https://www.facebook.com/lindyzart
http://lindyzartauthor.blogspot.com

Follow Lindy's Amazon author page here:
http://www.amazon.com/author/lindyzart